MIND IF I READ YOUR MIND?

HENRY WINKLER
AND LIN OLIVER

SCHOLASTIC INC.

New York   Toronto   London   Auckland
Sydney   Mexico City   New Delhi   Hong Kong

To the woman I share Ghost Buddy's imagination with, Lin Oliver, the best partner in the galaxy. And to Stacey always. —H.W.

For Henry, who has made creating our nineteen books together pure joy! —L.O.

ISBN 978-0-545-29883-4

12 11 10 9 8 7 6 5 4 3 2 1   12 13 14 15 16 17/0

Printed in the U.S.A.   40
First printing, July 2012

Designed by Steve Scott

CHAPTER 1

Billy Broccoli hung on to the mane of the horse as it hurtled wildly across the Sahara desert. A tribe of bearded nomads atop snorting, spitting camels galloped so closely behind him that he could feel the lead camel's hot breath on his neck. The leader of the pack, raising a double-edged sword that glistened in the blazing sun, shouted for him to stop, but Billy refused. As Billy held on to his white stallion for dear life, he saw a desert dust storm swirling toward him. He reached up to cover his face, but it was too late. The hot blast of air shot into his ear and traveled from one side of his head to the other. It felt like his brain was on fire, and he let loose a piercing scream.

"I give up!" he shouted. "You can have the treasure map. Just stop the hot air. I can't stand it anymore!"

He jumped from the saddle, flew through the air, and landed with a thud on . . . the carpet of his bedroom floor!

Billy stood up and looked around. He rubbed his eyes, trying to determine where he was. He saw no sand, no camels, no tribe of bearded nomads chasing him. Only Hoover Porterhouse, the ghost who shared Billy's room, floating above him and clutching his sides with laughter.

"What do you think you're doing?" Billy snapped, not sharing his ghostly roommate's amusement.

"I was bored waiting for you to wake up," the Hoove answered, "so I blew in your ear. Hey, it worked. Look, you're up."

"I was in the middle of a dream and now I'll never know how it ends."

"Well, I can tell you this. You were snorting like a camel and it was pretty disgusting. I had to put an end to it, for your own reputation."

"What kind of reputation? There's no one here but me and you."

"The Hoove's Rule Number Sixteen, Billy Boy. You always got to keep yourself sharp because you never know who's looking."

No sooner were those words out of the Hoove's mouth when a pebble struck the glass of Billy's bedroom window. Billy looked outside to see his neighbor and fellow classmate Rod Brownstone standing in the yard between their houses, holding what looked like a small version of a satellite dish. The big oaf was spying again.

Billy flung open his window and shouted, "What do you think you're doing pointing that metal thing at my room, Brownstone?"

"This metal thing, for your information, is the latest technology in extreme home voice recovery," Brownstone shouted back.

"In other words, you're spying on me."

"I'm protecting you, Broccoli. I got a report on my neighborhood scanner that wild animal sounds were heard coming from your bedroom."

"I told you that snorting thing you were doing was out of control," the Hoove said, floating over to Billy and leaning a transparent arm on his shoulder. "Even so, that doesn't give this doofus the right to invade my bedroom."

"*My* bedroom," Billy answered, whispering out of the side of his mouth so Rod Brownstone's device would not pick up the conversation.

"Do I have to remind you again that I was here first?" the Hoove asked.

It had only been three weeks since Billy's new blended family had moved into the old Spanish-style house on Fairview Street and Billy had made the life-altering realization that his bedroom was haunted by Hoover Porterhouse III, a fourteen-year-old ghost who'd been dead for ninety-nine years. Billy still hadn't gotten his head entirely around the situation. He felt that having his own personal ghost was not only creepy but unfair. Just because Hoover had been the original occupant of this room, Billy was now trapped with him. The Hoove couldn't leave the property until he proved to the Higher-Ups, whoever they were, that he could be a helpful and caring ghost. And who was he assigned to? Billy Broccoli, a flexible kind of guy, who was willing to accept a lot of changes. But being stuck with a ghost with major attitude was a lot to ask.

The Hoove didn't like Rod Brownstone spying any more than Billy did. He glided out the window into the yard and circled Brownstone, who was as muscular and buff as Billy was small and scrawny. Rod had a beefy hand on the earphones attached to his voice recovery device, holding them tightly to his head to listen for sounds that were none of his business.

"Let's see how your little machine likes this," the Hoove said to Rod, who of course couldn't hear or see him. Only Billy could. The Hoove reached into the back of the dish and pulled out a red wire and connected it to a yellow wire. When the two wires met, screeching static blasted out of the device and shot directly into Rod's earphones.

"Eeooowww!" he screamed, pulling off the earphones. "Eeeeeooooooooowwww!"

Billy couldn't stop himself from laughing. It was just what the big snoop deserved.

"Nice work," he shouted to the Hoove. "That got his attention."

Brownstone stopped screaming and stared at Billy.

"Who you talking to, Cheese Sauce?" he asked suspiciously. "We're the only two guys here."

"Who you calling not here?" the Hoove said. "I'll show you I'm here!" He grabbed Rod's earphones from his hand and wrapped them around his knee. "Just try to explain that."

Rod stared down at the earphones on his leg. This was not the first unusual thing that had happened to him while spying on the Broccoli-Fielding household. There had been other weird occurrences . . . a desk that vibrated on its own, a poster that spun on the wall, floating objects that seemed to come out of nowhere. Frankly, the whole place gave him the creeps. Rod decided to get out of there.

"You're strange, Broccoli," he called out. "I don't like what I see around here. And I'm telling you right now, you're officially under extreme surveillance."

"Extreme surveil all you want," Billy shouted. "You're not going to see or hear anything."

"But you're sure going to feel something," the Hoove added.

With a gleeful ghostly laugh, he flipped into his Swoosh mode, zoomed ahead of Rod, and pushed a flowerpot in his path. Rod instantly tripped over it and fell to the ground, ending up on his behind and with a daffodil up his nose. He got up, shot Billy a nasty look, and scurried off like a frightened bunny. It was not a good exit for a guy who prided himself on his secret spy skills.

The Hoove floated back into the bedroom where he and Billy exchanged a satisfied high five. But there was no time to gloat.

"Billy, honey, I'm leaving," Mrs. Broccoli-Fielding called out, sticking her head into Billy's room. "If you want a lift to school, you'd better get ready fast."

Billy's mother was the principal of Moorepark Middle School. Billy had transferred there three weeks before, when they moved into the house with his new stepfather, Bennett Fielding, and his daughter, Breeze. The last thing Billy wanted was to pull up in front of the school in the principal's car. No eleven-year-old in his right mind would consider that a good way to make new friends.

"Thanks anyway, Mom. I'll walk. Don't worry, I'll be on time."

As a person who understood the psychology of middle schoolers, Mrs. Broccoli-Fielding didn't insist. Instead, she just smiled at her son, reminded him that there was an English muffin staying warm in the toaster, and left.

"Good decision, Billy Boy," the Hoove said, snatching the T-shirt Billy had just pulled from his drawer. "First of all, I can't let you wear this. Hoove's Rule Number Three Hundred Forty. No T-shirts with pictures of panda bears. Especially ones with fuzzy noses."

"You have a rule for that?"

"I didn't, but I do now. Just made it up."

The Hoove went to Billy's drawer and pulled out a brown and blue striped shirt with no nose on it. "Second of all," he went on, "walking to school is good. Gives the ladies the impression that you're an independent kind of guy."

"What ladies?"

"Billy Boy, sometimes I think you are hopeless. I was referring to the ladies at school. Now put this shirt on, and let's get moving. I could use some exercise myself."

"And I could use you to stay home," Billy answered, picking up his hairbrush, then deciding his hair was just fine the way it was. The Hoove had only recently discovered that Moorepark Middle School sat within the boundaries of his family's former ranch, which meant he could go there as much as he liked. Billy thought he was there way too much.

The Hoove handed him back the hairbrush.

"Don't even think about leaving this room with that rat's nest you have going on up there."

"I know, I know," Billy said. "The Hoove's Rule Number . . . Number, I forget. 'Your hair is your crown. Keep it polished at all times.'"

"Or in your case, plastered down."

Billy checked the clock and saw that he only had fifteen minutes to brush his teeth, grab the muffin, leave the house, race to school, and get into his seat in Mr. Wallwetter's first-period English class. Billy was someone who did not like to get into trouble, so he sped into triple time, moving faster than he had ever moved in his life. He raced out the door, down the sidewalk, and made it to the front steps of the school with two minutes to spare. The Hoove, who rarely took no for an answer, followed him, doing somersaults through the air. As Billy reached the top step of the front entrance, he popped the last bite of muffin into his mouth and turned around so quickly he almost made himself light-headed.

"You can go now, Hoove," he said.

"Hey, how did you even know I was here? I was quiet as a mouse taking a snooze."

"I can smell you, remember?" Billy answered. "You smell like a carton of orange juice."

"Well, excuse me, mister. I don't believe I've ever criticized the way you smell. But now that you've raised the subject, let me just say that we're not talking orchids."

"I was just pointing out that I can smell when you're nearby."

"I'm going to take that as a compliment," said a voice next to Billy. He turned to see that Ruby Baker was standing next to him on the steps, with a smile as big as all of California. "I used my vanilla bean body lotion this morning."

Billy was not the kind of guy who would tell a girl that she smelled good. He didn't have any smooth moves like that. So he gulped and tried to come up with something to say to Ruby to cover his embarrassment.

"Vanilla is my favorite ice cream flavor," he stammered. "So I meant that in a very good way."

The Hoove gave Billy a big thumbs-up. It was the first time he had seen him talk to a girl without seeming like he was going to pass out from fear.

"Now tell her she smells like a banana split. With cherries on top."

Billy shook his head and gave the Hoove a get-out-of-here look.

"I'm telling you, it works," the Hoove insisted. "I once told Emma Ortiz she smelled like a freshly baked chocolate chip cookie, and she followed me around for months."

"Come on, let's walk to class together," Ruby said to Billy.

"You mean just the two of us?"

Ruby got a puzzled look on her face. "Who else is here?"

"Oh, you're right. No one." Then, looking in the Hoove's direction, he repeated, "*No one* but the *two* of us will be going to class now."

"Oh, so now I'm no one," the Hoove said. "Boy, if that doesn't fry my boots. You go out of your way to help a guy, get rid of snoopy intruders, make sure his hair doesn't look like a swamp, walk him to school in safety, and then in an instant, poof, I'm reduced to an invisible nothing. A grain of sand. What a ghost has to endure for mortals!"

Billy pretended he didn't hear the Hoove's rant and instead just headed up the stairs with Ruby, trying to think of something else to say. Mr. Wallwetter's class was on the second floor at the end of the hall, so he was going to have to fill the distance with some kind of conversation. To his relief, Ruby started talking about her three-mile run the day before, and Billy was happy just to nod.

The Hoove was offended to be brushed off like that, and in his anger, he stomped over to the flagpole in front of the school and kicked it. Had he been a live human, he would have hurt his foot, but being a ghost, his foot went right through the pole. Suddenly, a gust of wind blew so hard that the ropes on the flagpole twisted into a knot. A bolt of lightning, seemingly out of nowhere, struck the grass and carved out the word *NO* in giant capital letters. The Higher-Ups were not happy with Hoover.

"Oh, come on, you guys, give me a break!" the Hoove said, looking skyward. "I was insulted. Can't a ghost let off a little steam?"

A sudden clap of thunder gave the Hoove his answer.

"Okay, okay. I hear you. You don't have to yell," he said. "I'm trying to improve, and I swear I'll be more patient with the kid. Although, let me tell you, he pushes me to the limit. And might I add, his hair offends me."

Another angry clap of thunder sounded.

"Fine, I'll take care of him. I'll be sweet as homemade chocolate swirl ice cream with whipped cream and a cherry on top."

The ropes on the flagpole unraveled, the *NO* in the grass faded, and the knot disappeared. A long beautiful musical note that sounded like it came from a silver flute filled the air.

"Thanks for giving me another chance," the Hoove said. "I send you gobs of appreciation."

Had anyone been around to observe these strange events, they would have thought they were going a little ding-dong. Yet for the Hoove, there was nothing ding-dong about it. He regularly received messages from the Higher-Ups, who monitored his progress. Every so often, he got a ghostly report card, and he only had until the end of the year to pass all his required classes. He had passed Personal Grooming, Haunting Skills, and Invisibility, but he had failed Helping Others and Responsibility for the past ninety-nine years. If he didn't pass this year, he would be grounded for eternity and would never be able to leave the boundaries of the original ranchero where he'd lived and died. That meant he'd never be able to realize his dream of visiting all the baseball parks in America. And that was unacceptable.

The Hoove decided to calm himself down by visiting the school cafeteria. Although he hadn't had a real meal in ninety-nine years, he still loved the smell of meat loaf and brown gravy. He breathed it in, and the rich aroma seemed to soothe his anger.

Billy and Ruby hurried down the main corridor and arrived in Mr. Wallwetter's class just as the bell rang and Mr. Wallwetter began to speak. He wasn't one to start class even a second late.

"I have an exciting announcement today," he shouted over the bell. "Today marks the first day of the SOC."

Billy panicked. He looked down at his feet and realized that in his rush to get to school, he had forgotten to put on his socks. How was he going to explain that to Mr. Wallwetter, who seemed overly excited about socks? Fortunately for Billy, Mr. Wallwetter was referring to a different kind of sock.

"Every year, our school sponsors an important competition we call the Speak Out Challenge, known to those of us who love it as the S.O.C., or as we call it, SOC."

When Billy heard that the *K* was missing, the perspiration of fear behind his knees dried up immediately. However, he did make a mental note never to forget his socks again.

"Each one of you will give a public address on this year's topic," Mr. Wallwetter explained, "and the three best speakers from each sixth-grade class will participate in the finals to be held in the auditorium next Monday. I am proud to say my class has won the finals three years in a row. I am counting on it again this year."

Mr. Wallwetter was a thin man with a pencil mustache above his even thinner lips. He wore a black suit to school every day, and a tie so thin it could almost be called a shoelace. As he described the Speak Out Challenge to the class, his mustache started to sweat, which gave the appearance that his nose was running. Watching him work himself up into such a frenzied state about the competition made Billy shift uneasily in his seat. Everyone in the class felt the pressure, even Rod Brownstone.

"What are we supposed to speak out about?" Rod blurted. "Because I have a lot to say about law enforcement, especially the need to follow jaywalking rules exactly as they are written."

"That sounds like a noble pursuit," Mr. Wallwetter said, "but unfortunately it does not fit into this year's topic, which is *Demonstrate Something Special You Can Do*. Each of you is to give a speech while demonstrating something you love to do or can do very well. Now, who has a special skill they can demonstrate?"

Taylor Burnett, a shy boy who rarely spoke up, raised his hand tentatively.

"I can catch a Frisbee with my mouth," he said.

"What are you, a dog?" Rod guffawed. He laughed so loud he didn't notice that no one else was laughing. The kids liked Taylor and no one but Rod wanted to make fun of him.

"Now, people, let's break into groups and brainstorm topics," Mr. Wallwetter said. "You'll have a few days to prepare your speech, and then we'll begin the competition. Remember, second place is not an option in Wallwetter's World."

Billy got assigned to a group of five students. They all seemed to be brimming with ideas.

"I can run a mile in seven minutes and fifty seconds," Ruby Baker said. "I could demonstrate how I warm up."

"I can pull a quarter out of a person's ear," chimed in Zoe St. Clair.

"I can throw a knuckleball," Ricardo Perez offered, "or cook up a storm." Even though he was the star of the baseball team, Ricardo was the only person who had welcomed Billy on his first day at Moorepark Middle School. And there he was, being nice again.

"What's your thing, Billy?" he asked. "You look like a dude of many talents."

Billy's mind was racing but getting nowhere. Just the thought of standing up in front of everyone made his mind go blank with fear. He had always been that way about public speaking or performing in front of groups. In kindergarten, he had played a tube of toothpaste in the Halloween show, and when it was his turn, he couldn't remember how to pretend to squeeze himself onto the toothbrush, played by Vivian Pomerantz. So instead he just stood in front of the class and watched in horror as a lake formed around the zipper area of his pants. It took forever to live that down.

Even just the year before, at his old school, his throat closed up during Poetry Week when he had to recite "Casey at the Bat." It took three trips to the water fountain for him to finish the poem. He felt no confidence about being able to do well in the SOC competition. The old panicky feelings prickled every nerve ending from his hair roots to his toenails.

He sat in his brainstorming group with no sign of any storm whatsoever in his brain. Not even a raindrop of a thought. Suddenly, he smelled orange juice and felt a cold presence next to him. He looked up and saw Hoover Porterhouse standing on Mr. Wallwetter's desk, snapping his suspenders and doing the craziest dance he had ever seen.

"Tell them you can turkey trot with a ghost," he said. "Now that's a winning demonstration if I ever heard one."

Billy's stomach sank to the soles of his feet. This was not good. He was trying to fit in, to overcome his fears. And now here was the Hoove interfering again. The last thing he needed was a turkey-trotting ghost whispering in his ear. But making the Hoove understand that would be about as easy as balancing a tow truck on his little finger while singing opera in Italian.

In other words, impossible.

CHAPTER 2

It was South of the Border night in the Broccoli-Fielding household. Billy's new stepfather, Bennett Fielding, loved to cook and always had a theme for each meal. In the three weeks since Billy and his mom had moved in with Bennett and Breeze, they had already visited Italy via Bennett's lasagna, Japan through his chicken teriyaki, and Greece in the form of stuffed grape leaves and flaming fried cheese. The Greek night got a little out of control when the flaming cheese attacked the paper napkins and Mrs. Broccoli-Fielding had to douse the whole table with a pitcher of water. The family promptly traveled back from Greece to Jack in the Box for double cheeseburgers, which weren't as festive but were at least dry.

Billy had come home from school that day very tired after attending baseball practice. He was scorekeeper and never got to play, but sitting in the dugout and concentrating on each player's statistics had worn him out. He was in his room taking a pre-dinner nap when the door flew open and Bennett came dancing in. He was wearing a sombrero and shaking his hips in a very alarming way.

"*Hola*, Bill," he said. "Come into the kitchen where there is hot salsa to dip a chip in and hotter music to shake your body to."

Billy shook his head. He really liked Bennett most of the time, but right now he wasn't in the mood to travel to Mexico.

"I'll be there in a while, Bennett."

"No, no, señor. We need you now. There are ripe avocados calling your name, just waiting to be smushed up into guacamole."

Bennett danced over to Billy's bed and extended a hand.

"Come on, muchacho," he said. "Everybody helps."

With a sigh, Billy got up and followed Bennett into the kitchen. The table had been set using a colorful Mexican blanket as a tablecloth. Billy's mom was frying taco shells, and Breeze was browning the taco meat in a skillet. Bennett did a peculiar cha-cha over to the pan and took a sniff.

"No onions?" he asked. "You can't have taco meat without onions."

"I gave up on chopping them," Breeze said. "They made me cry, which made my mascara run, which is totally unacceptable."

"Where are the onion goggles?" Bennett asked, opening the drawer where he kept kitchen tools like lemon zesters and cherry pitters and hard-boiled-egg slicers.

"I don't know how to break this to you, Dad, but I did us both a favor and tossed those puppies out before we moved."

"You tossed out the onion goggles? Breeze, they're crucial. Why would you do that?"

"Three reasons, Dad. One, they smell like feet. Two, they made me look like an alien. And three, they were completely fogged up with onion fumes."

Bennett looked like he had lost his best friend. Billy knew the feeling. Before they moved, his mom had tossed out his collection of used chopsticks from his favorite Chinese restaurants, and he still missed them.

"Sorry about your goggles, Bennett," he said.

"I'll get you a new pair, honey," Billy's mom offered, leaving her taco shells to give Bennett a little hug.

"Those goggles and I have made a lot of salsa together," he said.

"Trust me, Dad. If I hadn't thrown them out, the Health Department would have. Even Brittany thought they were gross."

"Brittany Osborne?" Billy piped up, suddenly getting interested in the conversation. "The girl with the pink streaks in her hair. She thinks everything is gross."

"For your information, youngster, they are lavender highlights, not pink streaks. And she is the drummer in my band and one of my best friends, so I'd appreciate it if you wouldn't criticize her. Besides, the only things she ever said were gross were the onion goggles and you."

"I'm not gross."

"Really? Then what do you call that shriveled-up rotting tomato you're keeping on our bathroom counter?"

"I call it science. I'm watching that tomato decompose."

"Eeuuww."

"When fungi attack a fruit, it causes mold, which is why the tomato has turned black and fuzzy."

"Double eeuuww. Triple eeuuww. Everything eeuuww. That is the most disgusting thing I have ever heard in my whole life. You are officially the king of grossdom."

Bennett came to Billy's rescue.

"I applaud you, Billy," he said, taking the spoon from Breeze and stirring the meat so it didn't stick to the bottom of the pan. "Science is not always pretty, but a good scientist observes what's around him with an unwavering eye."

"And a strong stomach," Breeze chimed in.

Dr. Fielding certainly knew what he was talking about in the category of disgusting. He was a dentist, and he spent his whole day inside people's mouths. He knew all there was to know about tooth decay, gum disease, sour saliva, and bad breath.

As the four of them sat down at the dinner table, the family became very jolly. There was nothing like tacos and refried beans and fresh salsa to put a family in a great frame of mind.

Mrs. Broccoli-Fielding talked about how well the resurfacing of the new teacher parking lot was going. Dr. Fielding spoke enthusiastically about the new watermelon-flavored mouthwash he was experimenting with. Breeze reported that her girl band, the Dark Cloud, had been booked for the chess club dance party and although they weren't getting actual money, they got all the chocolate chess pieces they could eat.

Billy was quiet and didn't contribute much to the conversation. His mind had returned to the SOC contest. With less than twelve hours to go before first-period English, he still hadn't come up with a topic. He had already rejected at least five. His latest thought was to speak on how to stop yourself from hiccuping, but then he realized that standing in front of the room holding his breath would not make for a very upbeat presentation. Besides, if he passed out, he'd never live it down.

"Why so quiet, young William?" Bennett asked, helping himself to a third taco.

"I'm just thinking, and it's not working."

"Try using your brain," Breeze suggested. "Most people find that useful."

"Well, since *your* brain is working," Billy answered, "what did you do for the SOC competition last year? I can't think of a topic, and I'm starting to freak out about it."

"Our theme was *What It Means to Grow Up*. I set my speech to music and performed a song called 'My Nail Polish Doesn't Define Me.'"

"Yeah, I almost picked that" — Billy nodded — "but I rejected it. Hate to appear shallow, but my nail polish does define me."

Breeze didn't usually laugh at Billy's jokes, but this one seemed to tickle her fancy.

"Not bad," she giggled. "There may just be a funny human in there."

"So, Billy sweetie," his mom said as she stood up to clear her plate. "What topics are you considering?"

"It has to be a demonstration of something special I can do. The problem is, I can't do much. And even if I could, I'm not good at demonstrating."

"You can demonstrate taking a nap," Breeze said. "You seem pretty good at that."

"Nah, that would be a snooze," Billy joked again.

"That's two for you," Breeze giggled. "This dinner is more fun than I expected."

"I have the perfect solution," Bennett said, hopping to his feet and running toward the hall bathroom. He shouted over his shoulder, "Trust me, this will stun people. It will have them talking for weeks."

Billy and Breeze exchanged looks. What topic could Bennett find in the bathroom? The possibilities were endless . . . and disgusting. They didn't even dare to venture a guess.

Bennett returned grinning from ear to ear, and practically crashed into his wife, who was bringing chocolate pudding to the kitchen table. He held out two tightly fisted hands.

"Pick a hand, any hand," he said to the kids.

"How about neither?" Breeze answered.

"I say the left one," Billy said.

With a flourish, Bennett opened his left hand, and sitting in the middle of his palm was a plastic container of . . . minted, tinted dental floss!

"Your topic, Billy, is called . . . are you ready for this . . . wait for it . . . *Floss-O-Rama*."

"May I be excused?" Breeze said. "I've already seen this. He did it for my fourth-grade class on Career Day, and for the rest of the year, everyone called me Flossie the Tooth Fairy."

"Sit down, Breeze, and keep an open mind please," Mrs. Broccoli-Fielding said. "Bennett has so many wonderful ideas. I'm sure this one won't disappoint."

Bennett cleared his throat and stood at the head of the table. He flipped open the plastic container and pulled out a long strand of floss, wrapping the end of it tightly around his index finger.

"You'll start by explaining to your fellow students that one needs just the right amount of floss for perfect food removal," he began. "It can't be too short, or you won't be able to reach your back molars. If it's too long, it will sag. Tooth flossing is all about maintaining the proper tension."

Billy's jaw dropped open and Breeze's head hit the table. Only Billy's mom seemed to be thoroughly enjoying Floss-O-Rama.

Bennett snapped off a length of dental floss and wrapped the freshly cut end around his other index finger.

"Now," he said with a big smile, "I am ready

to begin the most important tooth ritual of the day. Billy, can I demonstrate on you?"

"Thanks for the offer, Bennett, but I have some chocolate-pudding action going on in my mouth right now and I don't think anyone at the table wants to see that. Especially in the lower left quadrant, where it's mixed with guacamole."

"And there we have the exact definition of Too Much Information," Breeze commented.

Bennett ignored both kids. He was not going to be stopped.

"Fine," he went on. "Then I'll demonstrate on myself."

He opened his mouth wide, plunged the thread of minty-green floss between his two front teeth, and wiggled it vigorously. Out of his mouth flew a tidbit of taco shell. It shot with surprising speed across the table, where it landed on the red stripe of the Mexican tablecloth. Rather than being grossed out by the sight of his already-been-chewed food, Bennett was ecstatic.

"Success!" he cried, with a little cha-cha step thrown in. "That little sucker was on its way to festering decay."

"Now it's just festering nausea," Breeze said. "As in mine."

"Don't listen to her, Billy," Bennett said. "I guarantee that you will be the only one in your class to give this demonstration, and trust me on this, it's a winner."

"No, trust me," said a voice coming from the ceiling. Billy looked up, and hanging off one of the blades of the ceiling fan was the Hoove, who had obviously been watching long enough to see the launch of the taco missile. "Flying food coming out of your mouth will end your hopes of anyone wanting to been seen with you in public until the year 2026."

"So what do you say, Bill?" Bennett said. "Is my idea great or is it great?"

"Can I add a third choice?" Billy asked.

"It better be, 'Are you out of your mind?'" the Hoove chimed in.

"Can I answer for myself, please?" Billy asked the Hoove.

"Of course you can, honey," his mother answered.

"Hey, Mamacita, he was talking to me," the Hoove said irritably. Billy was thankful that only he could hear the Hoove, because he knew his mother would have been offended. She insisted on everyone using a civil tone, no matter what the issue.

"Well, Bennett," Billy stammered. "I love your idea, I really do. But I'm afraid that it's so good, I couldn't possibly do it justice."

"Oooooh . . . look at Billy Boy go," the Hoove said approvingly. "Letting the good doctor down easy. Smooth as silk."

Billy stood up. "What I'd like to do, Bennett, is go to my room and determine if my public demonstration skills can rise to the challenge that Floss-O-Rama presents."

"Good thinking," Bennett answered. "And you won't want to forget this."

He tossed the plastic container of dental floss to Billy, and just as Billy reached out to catch it, the Hoove picked up a wooden spoon from the counter and, using it as a bat, swung and hit the dental floss across the room.

"Line drive!" he yelled.

Bennett ducked as the floss whizzed by his ear.

"Wow, Bill," he said. "I don't know how you got the spoon on that so fast, but if you put that same kind of focus on floss, you're going to win this competition hands down."

Billy just smiled and waved as he backed quickly out of the kitchen and headed to his room. Hoover followed close behind, making crowd cheering noises in Billy's ear and kissing himself all over.

"Did you see the way I smacked that thing? I told you I was a great ball player. If I hadn't crashed that car, I would have made the major leagues."

As for Billy, there was no cheering, no bragging, and no kissing of self.

He still didn't have a SOC topic.

CHAPTER 3

Billy paced back and forth in his room. He sat on his bed. He sat at his desk. He sat *on* his desk. Then he paced again. Nothing was helping. His mind was a total blank, except for the panic that was slowly creeping in.

"Stop pacing, will ya?" the Hoove said. "You're going to give yourself blisters on the bottom of your feet."

"Wait a minute. That's an idea," Billy said. "How about if I demonstrate that? I can just pace back and forth from one end of the class to the other until I get a blister."

"Knowing you, you'd cover it with a fluorescent yellow Band-Aid with teddy bears," the Hoove said, a noticeably sarcastic tone in his voice. "Besides, what if you didn't get a blister? Maybe you'd get a callus instead. Then where would you be?"

"Knock it off, Hoove. I'm working hard here to come up with something, and your negative comments aren't helping."

"Fine, do the dental floss thing. Go ahead and flick your breakfast morsels at everyone. See if I care."

The Hoove floated into Billy's closet and slammed the door behind him. He shoved Billy's hangers to one side to make more room for him to flop down and sulk.

"I had a lot more room in here before you hung up all your so-called fashion statements," he hollered through the door. Trying to find a comfortable spot, he dislodged a plastic laundry basket, and a load of unwashed socks tumbled out.

"Are you aware that the sweat in your socks has been multiplying in here?" he called to Billy. He would have held his nose, but there was no nose to hold. The smell was too much for him and he floated through the door back into Billy's room.

"Your socks smell like the cow pies we used to set on fire to keep the frost off the orange trees."

"I don't know what you're talking about, Hoove. What is a cow pie?"

"You modern city boys don't know the first thing about ranchero living. When my family lived here, back in the early nineteen hundreds, the orange groves stretched as far as you could see. Beyond that were the cows, who would leave behind steaming piles of . . . how should I say this . . . poop. Once it hardened, you got your pie. Now to set a cow pie on fire, all you gotta do —"

"Enough!" Billy interrupted. "Tomorrow morning is getting closer and closer, and unless I want to demonstrate setting cow doodle on fire . . . which, by the way, I'm totally not doing . . . I still have no topic."

Billy heard footsteps running down the hall. He could tell it was Breeze by the way she didn't knock as she stormed into his room.

"Thanks for not knocking," he said.

"You're welcome. Billy, I need to borrow a green marker. Mine disappeared."

Billy glanced suspiciously at the Hoove.

"Okay, I confess," the Hoove said. "I was doing a little drawing and forgot to put it back."

Billy reached over to the Dodger mug that he kept on the pink wicker desk he had inherited from the previous room's occupant, an eight-year-old girl. He looked through the pens and pencils in the mug and found a green marker.

"You can borrow it, but I want it back," he said to Breeze.

"Ten minutes. I just have to draw the letters of the alphabet for Colin Connors, this cute little first grader I'm tutoring. Green is his favorite color."

A sudden thought hit Billy. He turned to Breeze, almost hugging her but stopping himself just in the nick of time.

"Thank you, Breeze, a million billion gazillion times!"

"For what?"

"You said the word *alphabet*. You're a total genius."

"And you're a total weirdo," she shot back, shoving the green marker in her jeans pocket and backing out of Billy's room as fast as she could. "Oh, and don't call me, I'll call you."

"Hey, for once I agree with her," the Hoove said as soon as she was gone. "What was that million billion gazillion hiccup all about?"

"She gave me my topic, Hoove. My ticket to win. I can smell victory already."

"Do tell, which I wouldn't mind you doing because I have no idea what you're talking about."

"When Breeze said the word *alphabet*, it struck me like a bolt of lightning. Something my dad taught me before he and my mom split up. He showed me how to recite the alphabet . . . *backward!*"

"Billy Boy, please don't tell me that is what you're going to demonstrate. My ears definitely don't want to hear this."

"No, no, wait. Here's the amazing part. I can do it in less than fifteen seconds. How incredible is that!"

"Here is my answer, and it's got three letters. Give me an *N*. Give me an *O*. Give me a *T*. If I'm not mistaken, that spells *NOT*, as in NOT incredible."

"Wait until I show you."

Billy was already rummaging around in his desk drawer for the stopwatch his mom had bought him for his eighth birthday when he was into timing things, like how long he could hold his breath or sing a note or sustain a burp. He found it buried under his second-grade report on underwater volcanoes and pulled it out, tossing it to the Hoove who caught it with one transparent hand.

"Go ahead. Time me," Billy instructed him. "Push the top button as soon as I start."

"Have you started? This is so interesting I think I fell asleep."

"No, I haven't started, and stop kidding around. Click now."

The Hoove clicked the stopwatch and yawned. Billy took a deep breath and began. "Z . . . Y . . . X . . . W . . . V . . . U . . . I forget."

The Hoove clicked the button on the stopwatch. It read four seconds.

"If I'm not mistaken," he commented, "*I forget* is not a letter. And if it is, it doesn't come after *U*."

"Let me try once more," Billy said. "I'm just a little rusty. It's been a while."

"If you don't get it this time, I'm going to bed. This whole alphabet extravaganza is giving me a boredom rash."

Billy tried one more time and he got all the way to the letter *K*, but the attempt took him twenty-three seconds.

"Look at this," the Hoove commented when Billy was done. "My boredom rash is spreading. I've had it, pal. I am this close to suggesting you reconsider Floss-O-Rama."

"I'm going to get this, Hoove. You just wait and see."

"Well, as soon as you do, let me know. I'll be in the closet with a nose clip on." Hoover floated through Billy's closet door and settled down in the corner as far away from the socks as he could get. Through the wall, he could hear Billy repeating the alphabet over and over and over. After a few minutes, he thought if he heard it one more time, his head would explode, although that was impossible because his head wasn't really there in the first place.

Billy kept at it, though. He never lost patience with himself and never thought about giving up. Of all the things you could say about Billy

Broccoli, one thing you could never say was that he was a giver upper. After half an hour of practicing, he finally got the complete alphabet correct in seventeen and a half seconds.

"Did you hear that, Hoove?" he called into the closet. "I did it perfectly, and shaved three seconds off my last attempt. In another hour or two, I'll have it in less than fifteen seconds."

This was not what the Hoove wanted to hear. As a matter of fact, he was done listening altogether. Sticking only his head through the closet door, he said to Billy, "Is there anything I can say that will put an end to this right now? Because if you continue, you're going to drive me out of my skull and out of this room."

"You know what, Hoove? You're selfish. I'm so close. Instead of grumbling about it, you should be out here cheering me on."

"Easy for you to say, Mister Repeat Yourself. If you had to listen to what I've had to listen to tonight, you'd be exasperated, too."

"You're supposed to be helping me."

"You don't want to be helped."

"Who says I have to do everything your way?"

"I already told you the alphabet thing is a snore and a bore. And what do you do? Refuse to listen, that's what. You go right on your merry way, reciting that thing until my eyes spin and my ears shrivel up like raisins. A guy has limits. Even a dead guy."

"I'm not interested in your limits," Billy said, raising his voice impatiently. "I have to get this right before morning. You're not the one who has to be up there in front of everyone and be embarrassed. I am."

"You're right, Billy Boy. And guess what? I don't have to be *here*, either. So I'm going to leave you to your backward letters and your stopwatch, and go find someone who says things only once."

The Hoove's full body materialized out of the closet. He had grown very impatient with this kid. Without even so much as a backward glance, he shot across the room, through the window, and out into the night, leaving Billy with a perplexed look on his face and a stopwatch in his hand.

CHAPTER 4

It was an unusually foggy night for Los Angeles. A gray mist hovered just above the ground, and the lamps on Fairview Street cast an eerie yellow glow. Hoover drifted down the block, straining his eyes to see if anything interesting was going on that could eliminate the ringing memory of the backward alphabet. He saw a cat roaming through a half-open trash can, licking the remains from a tuna fish can.

"Trust me, kitty, your cat lady friends are not going to appreciate your fish breath when you're done," he said. "Personally, I would have gone for the half-eaten cheeseburger."

Even though the cat couldn't see Hoover, it certainly felt his presence. The hair on its back stood straight up, and with a giant yowl, it jumped out of the trash can and into the fog.

"No wonder they call you *scaredy-cats*," the Hoove hollered after it. "Don't get your undies in a bunch. I'm a ghost, for crying out loud, not a zombie."

As the Hoove floated by the Brownstone house, he noticed Rod sitting at a window seat in the living room, looking down the street with infrared binoculars. He looked frustrated, probably because the fog was impairing his view into other people's windows. The Hoove decided it would be fun to mess with Brownstone. Breaking off a small branch from the avocado tree growing in their front yard, he floated up to the window and waved the branch right in front of Rod's binoculars.

From Rod's point of view, it looked like the avocado leaves were suspended in midair with nothing holding them up. He pulled the binoculars down and rubbed his eyes with his palms. Seeing that his little prank was getting to Rod, the Hoove tore off two of the leaves and actually floated through the window to hold them up to the lenses of the binoculars. When Rod looked through them again, all he saw were veins of the green leaves.

"Amber!" he called to his little sister. "What have you done to my binoculars?"

Rod Brownstone was the kind of guy who would blame anyone for anything, whether it was their fault or not.

"I'm not even in the same room with you, you big moose lip," she shouted. "I'm in bed."

"You're the moose lip," Rod shouted back, in what might have been the most unimaginative retort in the history of the world.

Hearing the argument, Rod's dad came into the living room, boxer shorts pulled up to his chin and a can of diet root beer in his hand.

"Stop calling your sister names," he ordered Rod, "or you're grounded for the weekend."

The Hoove felt satisfied that he had sufficiently messed up Rod's night, and, dropping the avocado leaves, he sailed through the window and happily flew off down the street.

As always, he longed to go floating around the city looking for adventure, but his options were limited. The Higher-Ups' rules stated that until he proved himself, he could not leave the boundaries of his family's original ranchero where he'd been born and lived until he crashed Georgie's father's Model T car. That gave him about three blocks from Billy's house in any direction — enough to get to the middle school, to three of the six theatres in the Cineplex, and to Tony's Express Dry Cleaners (which he didn't need because ghosts don't sweat). He could get to the drugstore, but only to the shampoo and indigestion aisles. Sadly, the candy display was off-limits. Many an evening had he spent drooling over the Baby Ruths from afar.

The Little League field in Live Oak Park was one of his favorite destinations, but he could only go as far as the left field fence. The rest was out of bounds, which was a huge frustration for him. In life, he had been the star pitcher of the San Fernando Junior Cougars, and even as a ghost, he still itched to get on the mound and throw some fastballs. As he floated through the fog to the baseball field, he remembered how he had begged the Higher-Ups to give him another ninety feet so he could get to the pitcher's mound. But they were strict and not inclined to make deals.

When the Hoove reached the left field fence, he glided to a stop and gazed longingly into the outfield. There wasn't a lot to see because the fog was so thick. In the stillness and quiet of the night, his mind drifted back to Billy. He wondered if the Little Nerd Man was still reciting the alphabet backward. That was one extremely determined but highly annoying kid.

As the Hoove stared through the chain-link fence, his eyes started to play tricks on him. Was the fog forming something in the outfield, or was that actually a man stepping through the misty curtain? And if it was a man, where had he come from? It was as if he'd appeared out of nowhere . . . and he was heading straight for the Hoove. Hoover Porterhouse was quite used to scaring people, but now, oddly enough, he was scared by the sudden appearance of this strange presence. Before he could fly away, the man was standing in front of him with his hands on his hips, looking very annoyed.

"Hey, don't you move an inch, kiddo. I was sent all the way here just to see you."

If the Hoove hadn't been freaked out before, he certainly was now. Squinting through the fog, he saw an older man wearing a beat-up Yankees cap. His face looked very familiar.

"I was just leaving," he said to the man. "It's late."

"Oh yeah," the man answered with a chuckle. "It gets late early out here."

"Wow, Yogi Berra used to say that."

"Apparently, he still does."

The Hoove's eyes grew wide with disbelief.

"Are you telling me that you're him?" he asked. "That you're the legendary manager of the New York Yankees? The same Yogi Berra who's in the Baseball Hall of Fame?"

"I'm not here to talk about me, kiddo. I'm here to talk about you."

For once, the Hoove was speechless. He watched, fascinated, as Yogi approached him and grabbed the chain-link fence with both hands. He had a weathered face, round glasses, and ears that seemed just a little big for his head. He wore the number 8 on his pin-striped Yankees uniform.

"Were you sent here by the Higher-Ups?" the Hoove asked him suspiciously. "Because if you were, I already know what they told you to say."

"I don't take orders from nobody," Yogi answered. "I'm a team manager. I give orders."

"So what are you doing here?"

"That's a very good question. Six minutes ago I was at a Yankees reunion dinner, cutting into a medium rare steak in New York City and enjoying a Caesar salad on the side. And in the middle of a forkful, a pale guy in a velvet tuxedo taps me on the shoulder and says there's a kid with an attitude problem he wants to introduce me to. Next thing I know, I'm here in front of you, still chewing on a garlic crouton. I assume you're the kid with the problem."

"I don't have an attitude problem," the Hoove answered. "I'm supposed to help this kid, and he's so thickheaded, he won't listen to me. He's the one with the attitude problem. He didn't want to take my advice, so I left him there in his room, playing with his stopwatch."

"I see the problem already," Yogi answered. "You can observe a lot by watching. And what I see is a guy who's throwing down his glove before the game's over."

"Excuse me," the Hoove said, "but your sentences are taking a left when my ears are going right."

"When I was a player, and then a manager, I always used to say that baseball is ninety percent mental, and the other half is physical."

"That's one hundred and forty percent," the Hoove pointed out.

"The numbers ain't important, kiddo. You're missing the point. The point is that success is in your head. And if you're going to be successful with these so-called Higher-Up guys, whoever they are, you got to get out of your own stubborn self and help the kid. . . . What's his name, anyways?"

"Billy Broccoli."

"Tough break for him. I can see why he needs you to be there for him a hundred percent. And the only thing one hundred percent about you is that you're not."

"This math is numbing my brain."

"Well, get your brain around this, kiddo. Those Higher-Ups are telling you to help Billy Broccoli. That's your team assignment, your job. You have to deliver for the team, which means sticking with the kid to the end, even when it's frustrating or boring or annoying. In other words, it ain't over 'til it's over. Now if you'll excuse me, my steak's getting cold."

And with that, Yogi turned and walked back into the fog, disappearing as suddenly as he had appeared.

"Wait a minute," the Hoove called after him. "Don't go yet. I didn't even get to ask you what it was like to play in Yankee Stadium."

There was no answer.

"Hey, someday can I play for your team, Yogi?" the Hoove shouted into the fog.

"Not 'til you get it right, kiddo," came a far-away voice.

Whether he wanted to admit it or not, the Hoove sensed that Yogi was right. He was expected to stick it out, hang in there with Billy. And what had he done? Left the minute things got too annoying. And it wasn't the first time, either.

The Hoove knew what he had to do. Without another thought, he turned and headed back toward his house and the room he shared with Billy.

CHAPTER 5

Billy was sound asleep in his pink desk chair, still clutching the stopwatch. The hours and hours he'd spent practicing the backward alphabet had worn him out so much that he couldn't even change into his pajamas or make it to the bed. He had just passed out in his chair, visions of letters spinning backward in his head.

The house was dark when the Hoove arrived, except for a small reading light next to Bennett Fielding's side of the bed. While his wife slept, he liked to stay up late reading articles about mild to moderate tooth decay. Just for fun, the Hoove tapped on Bennett's window. When Bennett looked up, he saw nothing and assumed it was the wind blowing one of the orange tree branches against the window.

The Hoove was feeling frisky so instead of floating in through one of the house walls as he usually did, he flew up to the roof and stood at the edge of the brick chimney. Holding his body straight as a pencil, he jumped feet-first down the chimney and shot to the bottom, landing in the fireplace. He stepped out and checked his look in the mirror over the mantel.

"Perfect as always," he said to himself, snapping his suspenders with a confident air. "Hoover Porterhouse, you may be dead, but you are still the cat's pajamas."

The Hoove drifted down the hall to Billy's room and, floating through the closed door, found Billy asleep in his chair. He checked the stopwatch in Billy's hand. It was stopped at exactly fourteen and three-quarters of a second.

"The kid actually did it," he said to himself. "He's persistent. Boring, but persistent."

He gave Billy a little poke in the ribs, but since he was not made up of matter, Billy couldn't feel it. So he promptly blew in his ear, startling Billy awake.

"Hey," he said. "Why do you keep doing that?"

"I wanted to congratulate you. I see by the stopwatch that you did your alphabet thing in less than fifteen seconds. I don't know why you'd want to, but you made it."

"I only did it once before I fell asleep. That doesn't mean I can do it again."

"It doesn't matter, Billy Boy, because I can't let you continue. I am here to help, and in my official capacity, I have to tell you that this alphabet trick of yours is not something a live person should be caught dead doing."

"I'm doing it anyway, Hoove. I have no choice. I was desperate for a project and I didn't hear any helpful suggestions coming out of your non-mouth."

"Well, trust me on this, Billy Boy. If you stand up and do that thing, every kid in your class is going to think that you're one guy they don't want to get within ten feet of or that you'll bore them so much they'll fall asleep facedown in their cheese burrito."

"You don't know what they'll be thinking," Billy answered. "What are you, a mind reader?"

"As a matter of fact, that is one of the many talents I possess. But with a twist. My friend Ezra and I used to pretend we could read each other's minds to impress the ladies. Once when we were at the Fried Chicken Basket Social, I held my hands up to my head and told Madge Perkins that Ezra was sending me messages from —"

The Hoove suddenly stopped talking and his face lit up like a lightbulb had gone off in his head.

"Wait a minute, Billy Boy. This is genius. I've got to kiss myself." The Hoove actually leaned over and planted a kiss on each of his knees.

Billy scratched his head. "I don't get it, Hoove. What in the world are you talking about?"

"Your speech tomorrow . . . for, you know, that shoelace competition thing."

"Can't you get anything right? It's not called the shoelace competition. It's the SOC. As in Speak Out Challenge."

"Shoelaces, socks, what's the difference. They both go on the feet. What's important is that I just got an idea that's going to get you a first-place medal . . . or whatever there is to win."

"Better than reciting the alphabet backward in less than fifteen seconds?"

"Trust me, Billy Boy, this is not just the best idea in the world. It is interplanetarial. What you are going to demonstrate, with the help of a certain fascinating ghost I know, is your ability to read another person's mind, just like Ezra and I used to do."

"Hoove, that is impossible. I can't read minds."

"That *was* so true, Billy, until you met me. I am your vision into other people's thoughts. All you have to do is stand up in front of the class, ask a question, and listen carefully."

"Listen to what?"

"To *me*, my friend. Don't you see? I'm going to be there, being the eyes behind your head. Your audience can't see me, but I can see them and tell you what I'm seeing."

"Wait a minute. That's cheating."

"And your point is?"

"I don't know about how it was in your day, but nowadays kids get in big trouble for cheating."

"If they get caught," the Hoove shot back. "And might I remind you, Mr. Small Thinker, you will be the only one who can see me or hear me. Are you going to turn yourself in? I don't think so. Once again, Hoover Porterhouse the Third has come up with a foolproof plan. As in, you win."

Billy thought about what the Hoove was suggesting. Little by little, he felt his hesitation about cheating melt away as it was replaced with an image of his victory. He saw himself standing in Mr. Wallwetter's class, with thirty-four sets of eyes on him. He would wow them with his ability to read their minds. Sure, it was a trick, but did that really matter? For a brief and shining moment, he would be a winner. He could actually see the possibility of triumph flash before his eyes.

And he liked it. He liked it very much.

CHAPTER 6

"Who wants to go first?" Mr. Wallwetter said as soon as the bell rang. His intense eyes scanned the classroom like an eagle searching for a big, fat snake to eat. "Do we have a volunteer?"

"I nominate Cheese Sauce here," Rod Brownstone blurted out, pointing to Billy with his beefy index finger. Some of the kids in the class snickered, but Billy ignored them. Growing up with the last name of Broccoli, he had gotten very good at ignoring cheese sauce jokes.

"How about it, Billy?" Mr. Wallwetter said. "Want to be our first speaker in the Speak Out Challenge? SOC it to 'em, if you get my pun!"

Billy gulped. The Hoove still hadn't shown up, and without him, Billy's new speech wouldn't work. The Hoove was now the main ingredient in his mind-reading demonstration. Billy was going to have to stall until he arrived . . . that is, if he ever *did* arrive. He hoped the Hoove wasn't pulling another disappearing act like he'd done the night before.

"Thanks so much for the offer, Mr. Wallwetter," Billy said, using his most charming voice and sociable smile, "but I'd rather go last, if that works for you."

"It doesn't," Mr. Wallwetter answered tartly, tugging on his skinny little mustache.

"Then how about next to last? I can make that work."

"Come right up to the front of the class now, Billy," Mr. Wallwetter said in a way that didn't leave room for argument. "Show us all your demonstration."

Billy looked around desperately for signs of the Hoove, hoping that he had floated in and was hovering somewhere above the fluorescent lights. No such luck. Billy's heart raced with a combination of anger and nerves. The Hoove had sworn he'd be there when the opening bell rang. Promised. On his honor.

"The Hoove's Rule Number One Hundred Forty-Three," he had declared just that morning.

"When you count on the Hoove, you can count on the Hoove."

Yeah, right, Billy thought. *I'd do better counting on my fingers and toes.*

As Billy shuffled reluctantly to the front of the class, Rod made farting sounds with his mouth in time to Billy's steps. Mr. Wallwetter didn't seem to notice, though. He was busy writing Billy's name on the board, along with the topic Billy had handed him just before class.

A DEMONSTRATION OF MIND READING BY WILLIAM C. BROCCOLI.

"Check it out," Brownstone snorted. "I bet that *C* stands for *Cheese Sauce.*"

"Honestly, Rod, why don't you knock it off already," Ruby whispered to him. "It wasn't even funny the first time."

Billy smiled at Ruby and she smiled back. *Enjoy it while you can,* he thought. In about two minutes, that great smile of hers was going to vanish when he made a total dork of himself trying to demonstrate mind reading and coming up with zippo.

"Are you ready, Billy?" Mr. Wallwetter

asked, putting down the chalk and walking over to his desk.

"We were born ready, weren't we, Billy Boy?" came a ghostly voice from the back of the room. Billy looked up and there, sailing through the door in his hyperglide mode, was Hoover Porterhouse!

"I was about to give up on you, pal," Billy said aloud before he could stop himself.

Mr. Wallwetter, not knowing there was a ghost in the room, thought Billy was addressing him.

"Well, I'll never give up on you, pal," he whispered, coming over to Billy and giving his shoulder a reassuring squeeze. "Show us what you got, young man."

"Let's do this," the Hoove said. "We're going to make their heads spin."

And just to emphasize the point, he made his own head spin, doing exactly eleven three-sixty turns in one second flat.

Billy took a breath and began, just as he and the Hoove had practiced all night.

"Many people think mind reading is a mysterious art, but for me, it has always come naturally," he said. "Just by looking deeply at someone, I can tell what they're thinking."

"You know what I'm thinking, Cheese Sauce?" Rod shouted out. "I'm thinking your demonstration is going to stink up the place."

"That does it," Hoover said to Billy, his ghostly face turning red with anger. "We're going to put this mega-mouth in his place. Just watch what I can do."

The Hoove zipped to Rod's desk and peered over his shoulder. Rod's notebook was open to his English divider, but hidden in back of the first page, right under a practice paragraph on the proper use of semicolons, was a copy of *Modern Law Enforcement* magazine. The Hoove moved in closer to see exactly what Rod was reading. Rod shivered, never suspecting for a moment that the cold breeze he felt was caused by the presence of a ghost.

"Oh yeah, I got gold here," the Hoover hollered to Billy. "This knucklehead is actually reading an article on how close you can park to fire hydrants. Can you believe people write articles about that?"

Billy smiled. This was just the piece of information he needed.

"Let's use Rod Brownstone as an example," he continued. "It looks to everyone like Rod is thinking about the Speak Out Challenge. Is that right, Mr. Brownstone?"

"You got it, Snooze Head," Rod answered.

Billy closed his eyes and suddenly put his hands to his temples.

"I am concentrating on your thoughts," he chanted. "Send me your thoughts, Rod Brownstone."

"You are so lame," Rod snickered.

With great drama, Billy opened his eyes wide, and stared at Rod as if he had just seen a ghost (which, by the way, he actually had).

"Aha," he said. "I see your thoughts. You are thinking about . . . about . . . fire hydrants!"

Everyone laughed.

"My dog thinks about fire hydrants, too," Amanda Bickman said. "Just before he pees on them."

"Very funny," Rod said. He wasn't laughing at all.

Billy grabbed his head again, even more dramatically than the first time.

"Shhhh," he whispered. "I am inside the brain of Rod Brownstone. His thoughts are racing toward my mind. Getting louder. Taking over my own thoughts. Coming closer . . . closer . . . closer . . ."

Suddenly, Billy threw back his head with a snap.

"I have it!" he cried out. "Rod, you are thinking about fire hydrants and how close you can legally park to one without getting a ticket."

Everyone laughed again. They all knew Rod enjoyed law enforcement, but no one suspected how totally obsessed he was. It was preposterous to think that anyone at Moorepark Middle School would concern himself with the rules and regulations involved in parking near fire hydrants. They weren't even old enough to drive a car, let alone park one.

"Yeah, right," Rod said. "Fire hydrant parking. Like that's something I think about."

The Hoove got really close to Rod and, with a sudden movement, knocked his notebook off his desk. It fell on the floor, and the issue of

Modern Law Enforcement dropped out, open to the article about fire hydrant parking.

"Look at what he's reading," Amanda said, picking up the magazine article and holding it up to the class. "It's about fire hydrants!"

Everyone in class gasped. And so did Mr. Wallwetter.

"Billy, that's amazing," Amanda said, uttering out loud what the others were thinking.

Rod's face turned bright red, his expression a combination of anger and embarrassment. He grabbed the magazine and stuffed it back into his notebook.

"How'd you do that, Cheddar Breath?" he growled, squinting at Billy with his beady, suspicious eyes.

"Very well," Billy answered with a mysterious smile.

And giving a little thumbs-up to the Hoove, Billy took his seat as the class applauded.

"Thank you very much," the Hoove said, taking an invisible bow. With a jaunty wave of his cap, he did a backflip in the air, and zoomed effortlessly out of the window.

CHAPTER 7

It took a while for Mr. Wallwetter's class to settle down. The kids were buzzing about what an incredible feat Billy had pulled off. Everyone had a million questions.

"Have you always been psychic? Do you talk to dead people? Can you tell what I'm thinking right now?" they all asked at once.

The buzzing continued until Mr. Wallwetter put an end to it by rapping three times on the edge of his desk with a ruler. That was his signal that everyone had to be quiet or he'd start writing names on the board. If you got your name on the board more than three times, you got sent to detention. Mr. Wallwetter did not like a noisy classroom.

"You should have your own TV show," Ava Daley whispered to Billy.

"I could loan you my cape and turban,"

offered Miles Galbraith. "I was a mind reader last Halloween."

"Thanks, guys, but I'm not good enough to be on TV," Billy whispered back modestly, though he was secretly thrilled with all the praise. His speech had done exactly what he'd hoped it would. His classmates were impressed. Very impressed.

Mr. Wallwetter put down his ruler and continued with the presentations, but everyone agreed that the rest of the SOC speeches couldn't compare to Billy's. Alex Flannigan demonstrated how to shoot a bow and arrow, but since Mr. Wallwetter did not permit him to use an actual arrow, he had to use an unsharpened pencil, which immediately slipped off the bowstring, flopped into the wastebasket, and disappeared. Reshma Patel demonstrated how to make an Indian curry, but her eyes watered so much when she shook the cayenne chili powder into the mixing bowl that she had to be excused to go to the girls' bathroom to splash water on her face. When she returned half an hour later, her eyes were as red as the cayenne pepper.

The other demonstrations were more average than average. Cecilia Gomez showed how to crochet a miniature cow, which looked more like a squirrel without a tail. Stephen Lowry did a Rollerblading demonstration up and down the aisles until he crashed into Mr. Wallwetter's model solar system, splitting Saturn in half. Jenny Yee showed the class how she puts in and takes out her contact lenses, which went fine until looking at her inner eyelids made Bobby Belenchia so nauseous he had to put his head between his knees.

The biggest surprise was Ricardo Perez's demonstration. Since he was the star player on the baseball team, Billy was positive that he would demonstrate his batting techniques or his knuckleball pitch. Instead, Ricardo showed the class how to make a carrot raisin salad. And when he passed out samples to the class, Billy was amazed at how delicious it was. Ruby Baker did something equally amazing when she showed everyone how she warmed up for cross-country or track and field events. She was so flexible that when she twisted herself around in her bright yellow warm-ups, she looked like a pretzel covered in mustard.

The lowest point of the hour was Rod Brownstone's demonstration of how to crawl behind enemy lines without becoming a blip on the radar screen. He slithered along the classroom floor like a reptile, and no one could see him unless they stood up, which no one bothered to do. There was one positive outcome of his demonstration — he did leave the classroom floor a lot cleaner. He even managed to pull a stuck piece of gum off the linoleum. A bunch of the girls snickered at the gum and dirt and grime on his belly. But in his usual overconfident manner, he strutted by them and said, "You're laughing now, but wait until I take first place in the finals."

That wasn't going to happen, though, because Mr. Wallwetter selected the three finalists right then and there. They were Ricardo, Ruby, and none other than . . . yes . . . Billy Broccoli!

Billy was overjoyed. On his way out of class, all the kids gave him a fist bump and told him how great his speech was. Everyone wanted to know how he did the mind reading, and for a fleeting second, he felt a little guilty. But the feeling didn't last long because everything he ever wanted at Moorepark Middle School was happening.

Ricardo invited him to sit with the baseball team at lunch, not as the assistant scorekeeper who sat on the end of the bench, but next to him, as the cool guy who had amazed their class. Michael Andrews said that maybe they could catch a movie sometime, especially if Billy could tell him the ending before they actually saw it. Reshma Patel asked him to dinner at her family's Indian restaurant, and said she was sure her father would give him free chicken tikka masala if he would do a little mind-reading demonstration for their customers.

Billy felt great, like he belonged and was finally being accepted. He couldn't wait to tell the Hoove.

In the hall on the way to math, he passed Breeze, who was standing at her locker with Ruby's sister, Sofia, and the other members of her band, the Dark Cloud. Word of Billy's dazzling feat had traveled fast, but Breeze couldn't believe that the amazing Billy everyone was talking about was the same Billy who made frog noises in the shower.

"Look who's here, the new school hero," she said, stepping away from her friends. "How did you manage that?"

"I have my talents," Billy said. "You don't know every single detail about me."

"Well, the one detail I do know is that you're not a mind reader." Breeze turned back to her locker and popped it open. Billy blinked twice when he looked inside. There, hanging on the coat hook next to Breeze's red velvet hat was Hoover Porterhouse. That guy was everywhere.

"I don't suppose you want to tell her the truth," he said to Billy. "That it's me who's the mind reader. Me who should be the new school hero."

Breeze sniffed the air. The pungent smell of oranges wafted out of her locker. Sofia shot her a strange look.

"Smells like somebody's orange juice carton sprung a leak," she said.

"That's not possible," Breeze answered. "I didn't pack any orange juice in my lunch."

Hoover Porterhouse laughed. "I love driving the girls crazy," he said. "It's what I do best. Other than mind reading, that is."

Breeze, who was a little embarrassed by the aroma coming from her locker, slammed the door shut.

"By the way," she said to Billy, "I'd appreciate it if you could make yourself scarce after school today. Sofia and I are working on some new songs for the band, and sixth-grade brothers are not invited."

"Oh, he can come," Sofia said. "Maybe he'll show us some of that fancy mind reading he does."

"No, he can't come," Breeze insisted. "I have dibs on the basement."

"That's fine with me," Billy said. "It's important for everyone's mental health that we keep your music down there anyway. Last time you hit that high note on your guitar, you nearly broke every glass in the kitchen cupboard."

Billy heard a hollow voice shouting at him from inside Breeze's locker.

"Turn around, Billy Boy," the Hoove called out. "You're going to like what you see."

Billy whipped around and saw Ruby approaching him with that great contagious smile of hers.

"I have a good idea," she said to Billy. "Want to hear it?"

"My ears are ready."

"How about if the three of us get together after school today?" she suggested. "You and me and Ricardo. We can plan how we're going to work together at the SOC finals on Monday. I was thinking maybe we start by introducing each other."

"That's a great idea, Ruby," Breeze said. "But our house is off-limits after school."

"Well, we can't do it at my house," Ruby said. "Our dad is working at home today and he needs quiet. I talked to Ricardo, and his mom has a cold and doesn't want anyone over. So that leaves your house."

"Which is not available," Breeze stated firmly.

"Don't let her get away with that," the Hoove yelled, sticking his head through the metal locker door and meeting Billy eye to eye. "It's *our* house, too. Let her stay downstairs. We'll take the upstairs. You guys can practice in the kitchen or in the living room or on the ceiling. Oh, wait, I'm sorry. That's just me."

Billy nodded at the Hoove and turned to Ruby.

"We'll do it at my house," he said. "Breeze and the band can practice in the basement. There's plenty of room upstairs, and if the music gets too bad, we can wear earplugs."

"Great," Ruby said. "Let's meet at four o'clock. Sofia and I will walk over together. If you see Ricardo, let him know the plan."

She turned and headed down the hall, looking like a bouncing lemon drop in her yellow sweats. Billy couldn't believe this was all happening. The SOC finals on Monday. An after-school rehearsal with Ruby and Ricardo. A hall full of kids passing by and shouting out their respect. As the bell rang and he raced off to math class, he told himself that this was a day to remember.

CHAPTER 8

Billy hurried home after school, his mind over-flowing with ideas. It was his first official after-school get-together with his new friends, and he wanted everything to be perfect. He had decided to make three different kinds of peanut butter snacks — peanut butter on celery, peanut butter on round sesame crackers, and peanut butter on thickly sliced bananas. Ruby and Ricardo would be there at four o'clock and he had a lot of peanut butter to spread before then.

He ran the last block to his house and unlatched the back gate, making his way to the kitchen door. As he passed the big oak tree in his yard, he heard the whistling sounds of "I've Been Working on the Railroad" coming from the top branches. That was the Hoove's favorite song, the one he whistled when he was trying to make himself visible. Billy looked up and saw one transparent arm dangling down from a branch.

"Where's the rest of you, Hoove? That looks really weird."

"I wouldn't be so quick to judge," the arm answered. "Materialization is not an easy process to master. It takes a special kind of concentration, and I'm a little distracted by that squawking blue jay over in Mrs. Pearson's yard."

"Mrs. Pearson's yard is five houses away."

"And there lies another difference between you and me. I can hear things up to a mile away, where you humans only hear what you want to hear. This particular blue jay is in a very bad mood and he's getting on my nerves. Somebody should throw him a worm and shut him up."

"Listen, Hoove, I'm in a hurry. I've only got fifteen minutes before Ricardo and Ruby arrive, and I have a lot to do. I could really use your help cleaning up my room."

"What do I look like, your personal butler?"

"Actually, you look like an arm, which is creepy."

Suddenly, the Hoove's whole body appeared. He lay stretched out lazily on the tree limb. His hat rested on a stubby offshoot of the branch, and his dark hair was coiffed in perfect movie star style.

"I think your little insult did the trick," he said. "Focused my energy and presto, here I am in all my glory."

"Good, now could you please get your glory in the house? I want to rehearse there. It's bad enough that I'll have to explain the pink furniture and rainbows on the walls. I don't want to have to apologize for a mess, too. I hope you can get it looking decent in fifteen minutes."

"Are you kidding me? If I flipped into hyperglide, I could have that room in tip-top shape in less than fifteen seconds. Faster than you can say the alphabet backward."

"Great!"

"That is, if I'm in the mood. I just said I *could* do it, I didn't say I *would*."

As soon as those words left the Hoove's mouth, a large blackbird with fierce orange eyes shot from the sky. It flew directly over the Hoove's head, let out a caw that sounded like "Help him!" and then released a large goop of poop, which landed squarely on top of the Hoove's movie star hair.

Billy roared with laughter, but the Hoove wasn't amused. He looked up into the sky.

"Was that really necessary?" he called to the Higher-Ups. "You could have asked me nicely."

The bird circled overhead one more time, keeping its eyes focused on him.

"Okay," he said. "I'll clean the kid's room. But this better get me a good grade in Helping Others, because I definitely do not appreciate bird waste."

"Just put everything away in drawers," Billy explained. "Pile the papers neatly on my desk, make the bed, and if it's not too much trouble, there's a vacuum cleaner in the hall closet."

"You want me to vacuum? Whoa, now you've stepped over the line." Then he looked up at the clouds and shouted, "You can send all the poop bombs you want. The Hoove does not vacuum. That's Rule Number Two Hundred Seventy-Eight. Oh, and while we're at it, Rule Number Two Hundred Seventy-Nine. I don't do windows, either."

Billy raced into the kitchen and got busy. He wished he had earplugs to drown out Breeze and her drummer, Brittany Osborne, who were already down in the basement working on a new song. They called it a song, but to Billy it sounded like one of them had hit her finger really hard with a hammer. At least he had the kitchen all to himself. He took the peanut butter and crackers out of the cupboard and a knife out of the drawer. The celery was in the refrigerator and the bananas were in a bowl on the counter. While he got to work slicing, dicing, and spreading, the Hoove flipped into hyperglide and zoomed down the hall into Billy's room.

From the Brownstone house next door, Rod's younger sister, Amber, stared out the living room window. She got up and pressed her face against the glass.

"Hey look," she said. "There are clothes flying through the air in Billy Broccoli's room. They look like rockets."

Rod Brownstone was watching afternoon cartoons on TV and eating Flamin' Hot Cheetos dipped in extra hot sauce. He was also drinking a lot of water because his lips were on fire. He didn't even look up from the TV.

"You should really look at this, Rod," Amber

said. "Wow, now the bedspread is floating across the room like a magic carpet."

Her brother grunted.

"Right, and I suppose Aladdin and the beautiful princess will be all kissy wissy smoochy on the magic carpet. Get a grip, Toad Breath. Your girly imagination is so annoying."

"Okay," Amber said. "I guess you don't want to see his bed bouncing up and down like a trampoline, either."

"What I want is for you to go away so I can watch my cartoons in peace." Rod popped another Cheeto in the hot sauce and turned his back on one of the most amazing sights Amber had ever seen.

By the time the front doorbell rang, Billy had finished making the peanut butter snacks and putting them on a platter decorated with seashells. He ran to the front door where Ruby and Sofia were waiting. Sofia carried her bass guitar in a black case covered with stickers from cities she had never been to. Before Billy could even say hi to Ruby, Breeze came up from behind, pushed right by him, and pulled Sofia into the house.

"It's so great you're here," she said, practically flattening Billy to the wall. "Brittany's already downstairs. She brought her drum pads over, and her beats inspired me to write some new lyrics. We can't wait to hear what you think."

Breeze and Sofia hurried into the kitchen. Just before they headed down the stairs to the basement, Breeze spotted the platter with Billy's peanut butter snacks.

"Hey, look what Billy made for us," she said, grabbing a few bite-size pieces.

"Billy did not make them for you," Billy said, following them into the kitchen with Ruby close behind. "And please leave the rest alone."

"Oh really?" Breeze said. "Seems to me that when you blend a family, you also blend everything that is edible, including but not limited to, all peanut butter products."

"I made those for my friends, Breeze. You could have thought ahead and made something for your friends."

"We're musicians, not food handlers," she answered with a mouthful of celery. "Come on, Sofia. Brittany is waiting. Besides, this stress isn't good for my creative process." Just before she started down the basement stairs, she turned around, opened her mouth wide, showing Billy the mush of half-chewed celery bits stuck together with peanut butter on her tongue, and said something that sounded like, "Do you want it back?"

"Yes, I do," Billy said, just to be contrary. "You can put it on a paper towel over there."

Ruby burst out laughing. She didn't have any brothers, so there was never talk of already-been-chewed food in her house. Over the sound of her laughter, Billy heard the chimes of the doorbell, which played "La Cucaracha," an old Mexican folk song. He was embarrassed that their doorbell wasn't regular, but then nothing about this old ranchero house was. Why couldn't their doorbell go *ding-dong* like everybody else's in the neighborhood?

"Sorry about the weird doorbell," Billy apologized when he opened the door for Ricardo.

"Are you kidding me, man? It's so cool. My grandmother used to sing me to sleep with that song. It worked until I found out that *la cucaracha* means cockroach. What kid wants to fall asleep dreaming of cockroaches?"

Billy led Ricardo into the kitchen, where Ruby waited for them. They sat down at the table and dug into the remaining snacks.

"We should probably lighten up on these," Ricardo said, "if we're going to practice our speeches. It's hard to talk with peanut butter in your mouth."

"Just one more before we start," Ruby said.

Billy picked up the platter to offer Ruby another snack of her choice. Just as she was taking one, he noticed a peanut butter cracker leave the plate and float by itself under the table. Pretending to have dropped something, Billy peeked underneath the table. Sure enough, there was the Hoove, holding the cracker up to his nose.

"What are you doing?" he whispered, dropping to his knees and crawling under the table. "You can't even eat."

"I know," said the Hoove, "but I love the smell of peanut butter. I couldn't resist."

Before Billy could answer, Ricardo stuck his head under the table. "What'd you drop?" he asked.

"Oh . . . a . . . cracker," Billy said, turning

quickly away from the Hoove. "My mother gets crazy if I leave crumbs behind."

"That's right, Billy Boy, just ignore me," the Hoove called, his tone a little irritated. "I'm only your best friend."

Without even a glance, Billy snatched the peanut butter cracker from his hand and turned to Ricardo. "Here it is. What do you say we get started?"

Billy stood quickly and pulled Ricardo up with him.

"Fine," the Hoove called out. "Have fun with your new friends. Just think of me as your personal room cleaner-upper. If you need any more favors, you know where to find me."

Billy sat down at the table and pulled out his notebook. Ruby was already writing down some suggestions in hers.

"I think I've worked out the order," she said. "I'll go first, then Ricardo, then Billy. You should go last, Billy, since your demonstration is the most amazing."

Before Ruby could go any further, the wail of a jarring guitar chord reverberated from the basement.

"Breeze," Billy shouted down the stairs. "It sounds like a porcupine got caught in your guitar strings."

"Get used to it," Breeze shouted back. "How do you think music is made?"

"Definitely not like that!"

Ruby tried to go on with what she was saying, but the musical screeching continued. In fact, it got worse when Sofia started to sing in her high-pitched, off-key voice.

"Sofia," Ruby screamed, "you sound like you're in pain."

"I'm supposed to," Sofia yelled back. "We're expressing the angst of being a teenage pebble in the driveway of life."

Ruby rolled her eyes at Billy and Ricardo.

"She always says stuff like that." Ruby shrugged. "My mom and I just pretend to understand."

Billy couldn't take it anymore.

"Honestly, you guys," he called into the basement. "Knock it off. We have a competition to win, and we need to practice without you screeching like a bunch of ghosts on Halloween."

The Hoove popped up from under the table.

"I resent that remark," he said. "I do not screech. People are always accusing us ghosts of howling and saying 'BOO,' and I'd like to put an end to that rumor."

"I wish," Billy said, casting a glance toward the Hoove, "that *someone* would put an end to their rehearsal."

"I can try," Ricardo said.

"No, I didn't mean you."

"Don't look at me," Ruby said. "I don't want to go down there and face my sister, especially when she has a microphone in her hand."

Billy shook his head and stared in the Hoove's general direction.

"Oh, so I guess that means me," he said. "Okay, okay. Once again, Hoover Porterhouse to the rescue. It seems I'm good enough to save the day, but not quite good enough to sit here and sniff the essence of peanut butter with you and your new best friends. Fine, I know my place."

And with that, he disappeared down the stairs to the basement, his ghostly form sliding down each step like a river of smoke.

CHAPTER 9

Breeze, Sofia, and Brittany were in the middle of composing a new song. It was called "Pity the Prom Queen," and it was the tragic story of a girl who was voted prom queen because of her beautiful smile, but her feet smelled so bad that no one danced with her all night. The Hoove listened to them practice. He liked the beat of the song, but he couldn't relate to the lyrics since he had never been to a prom or known a girl whose feet smelled that bad. Except for possibly Madge Perkins, whose father tended to the ranchero's orange groves. Her pet squirrel slept in her left boot every night during the winter, and by February the squirrelly smell was pretty harsh.

The Hoove glided down the basement stairs, unsure exactly how he was going to get the girls to stop rehearsing. At the bottom, he elongated his body like Elastoman and stretched around the corner to survey the scene. He noticed that the washing machine had a pile of dirty clothes stacked on top, waiting for their turn. An idea flashed into his mind. If that machine started up all by itself, that might be enough to send the girls screaming up the stairs and end the rehearsal. He had never done a load of wash before, but how hard could it be?

Floating over to the washing machine, he scooped up the clothes, lifted the lid quietly, and threw them in. He took a box of detergent from the shelf above the machine and poured the entire contents in. Closing the lid, he switched the machine on, then sat down on top of it and waited for the low rumble to start.

When the girls heard the washing machine filling with water, they looked at one another with surprise.

"Did you turn that on?" Sofia asked Breeze.

"No. I've been sitting here right next to you. What about you, Brittany?"

"How could I? I'm holding drumsticks in both hands."

The girls were quiet for a moment. The Hoove, enjoying their confusion, waited for them to scream and take off. But that didn't happen.

"Maybe my dad rigged it to a timer." Breeze shrugged. "He likes gadgets."

Before long, the washing machine had filled with water. The Hoove noticed suds bubbling up so fiercely that they were pushing the lid open and spilling out from the top of the machine.

"Whoa," he said to himself. "Maybe I overdid it, putting in the whole box of detergent."

But it was too late. Suddenly, soap suds exploded from the machine like an erupting volcano, oozing their way along the floor to where the Dark Cloud girls were sitting. Brittany noticed the approaching wave of foam.

"Maybe your dad should give up clothes cleaning and stick to teeth cleaning," she said.

Breeze dashed over to the washing machine and turned it off, but the soap suds just kept on coming. They were forming a thick carpet of foam that was heading directly to where the girls had set their guitars.

"Sofia, grab the instruments and run upstairs," Breeze said. "Brittany, get your drum pads. I'll rescue the lyrics."

The Hoove was enjoying the scene tremendously. He hadn't planned the soap suds disaster, but it had certainly gotten the girls to stop rehearsing. Other ghosts might have just tied their guitar strings in knots or taken the batteries out of their microphone, but not him. He had style even when he wasn't trying to have style.

Just as Breeze, Brittany, and Sofia arrived in the kitchen clutching their instruments and their soggy lyrics, Mrs. Broccoli-Fielding walked in the back door. As always, she clutched a briefcase overflowing with work.

"Hi, everyone," she called out. "What a nice surprise."

"We're just leaving, Mom," Breeze said. "We're going to practice at Brittany's house. And if you really want a surprise, check out the basement."

"But before you do," Sofia added, "put on your bathing suit."

Mrs. Broccoli-Fielding didn't understand what was going on, but nevertheless, she cheerfully waved good-bye to the girls as they raced out the back door. Then she plopped her heavy briefcase down, kicked off her red cowboy boots, and turned her attention to Billy, Ricardo, and Ruby.

"I bet I know what's going on here," she said with a big grin. "I saw Mr. Wallwetter in the faculty parking lot, and he told me the great news. I'm so happy to have his three SOC finalists at my kitchen table. Oh, and who made the lovely snack platter? I don't mind if I do."

Reaching for a banana and peanut butter slice, she popped it in her mouth.

"Tell me all about your topics," she said.

"We'd love to, Mom, but we're being invaded by a mountain of bubbles."

"Billy, honey, what on earth are you talking about? What has gotten into you and Breeze today?"

"It will become all too clear as soon as you look in your basement," Ricardo said. He didn't want to come right out and tell her the bad news. After all, he was talking to the principal of his school, and no one ever wants to make the principal angry for any reason.

Mrs. Broccoli-Fielding went to the basement door and looked down at the sea of bubbles steadily creeping up the stairs.

"What happened here? Who did this?"

"We don't know," Ruby said. "Breeze and her friends were rehearsing down in the base-ment. Maybe they turned on the washing machine."

"We can rule Breeze out," Billy's mom answered. "She would never volunteer to do the wash. And Sofia and Brittany have always been the perfect guests. So who's responsible for this?"

Billy put two and two together, and it only added up to one thing. "The Hoove," he mut-tered out loud before he could stop himself.

Everyone in the room turned to stare at him.

"What did you say?" they said in unison.

"Um ... I said, we better *move*," Billy answered.

"Excellent idea," Billy's mom said. "You kids take your rehearsal into Billy's room, and I'll call the plumber. Right after I have one more of those delicious banana and peanut but-ter slices."

Mrs. Broccoli-Fielding picked up the phone and called Clogged Pipes R Us Plumbing Service. She had a little trouble describing the situation to Mario the plumber because the peanut butter held her tongue to the roof of her mouth.

"I have *thuds* from the *bathement* coming up the *thairs*," she tried to explain, as clearly as she could.

Billy, Ricardo, and Ruby quickly gathered their notes and papers from the kitchen table. On the way to his room, Billy glanced down into the basement just to see how bad it really was. To his shock, he saw the Hoove diving in and out of the suds like a dolphin in the ocean, spraying bubbles in every direction. When he scooped up a handful of bubbles and plastered them to his face, the Hoove looked like a transparent Santa Claus with no bowlful of jelly.

"Come on down," he called to Billy. "This is a blast! Where have these bubbles been all my life?"

"All I asked was that you get the girls to stop playing!" Billy whispered to him. "Not that you make my house into one giant bubble slide."

"You know what your problem is," the Hoove said, doing a backstroke down the bubble-covered stairs. "In the car of fun, buddy boy, you have four flat tires." And with that, he did a flip and disappeared into the basement that was now a foaming, frothy pool.

Ruby had already reached Billy's room, plopped herself in his desk chair, and started to organize the notes she had taken. Ricardo moved Billy's sweatshirt from the spare chair in the corner and pulled it over, while Billy perched on the edge of the desk.

"So," Ricardo said, looking around at the walls and furniture. "Who's the pink and lavender fan? Please tell me it's not you."

"I inherited this room," Billy answered.

"I remember that unicorn wallpaper," Ruby said. "I had it when I was six."

"Listen, man," Ricardo said, putting a friendly hand on Billy's shoulder. "A word of advice. You might want to change the color scheme before you invite the rest of the baseball team over."

"Down to business," Ruby said, adjusting the yellow headband in her hair, which was something she automatically did when she got serious. "We have a competition to win here, gentlemen. What should we do first?"

"I think we should do our speeches for one another and make suggestions," Ricardo said. "That's what coach does at batting practice."

"You go first," Ruby said, turning to Billy, "because let's face it. Your speech is going to win this for us."

Ruby and Ricardo settled into their chairs, waiting for Billy to begin. He just looked at them uneasily, the long silence filling the room. At last, he spoke.

"I've been thinking," he began slowly.

"Always a dangerous move," Ricardo said.

"Good one!" Billy laughed, a little too loudly and much too long. Ruby gave him a funny look. Ricardo's joke wasn't that funny, but Billy needed the time to formulate his next sentence.

"I've been thinking that I'm ... I'm ... really thirsty."

"We just drank a ton of lemonade," Ricardo commented. "You have a powerful thirst."

"It's a mind reading thing," Billy explained. "Your brain has to be hydrated in order to ... um ... receive ... um ... you know." That sounded lame even to him, but without waiting for an answer, he turned and bolted frantically from the room, leaving Ricardo and Ruby exchanging a perplexed look.

Billy dashed down to the basement.

"Hoove," he called down. "You there? I need you."

A head popped up out of the bubbles, but it wasn't the Hoove. It was a curly-haired man wearing a yellow rain slicker over a pair of rubber fishing waders. He looked like he was dressed to do a hurricane report on the news.

"Who are you?" Billy asked.

"Mario the plumber, at your service. If you're looking for a friend, there's no one down here but me."

"Mario, you didn't happen to smell any orange juice down there, did you?"

"That's about the only thing I didn't smell, kid."

"Just one more question," Billy said. "Did you see anything floating through the air, like a cracker with peanut butter on it?"

"If I saw something like that down here, kid, I'd be up there with you."

"Okay," Billy said. "But if you suddenly smell orange juice or see something floating by, let me know right away."

"You'll be the first person I tell, right after I call the loony bin."

As Billy hurried back up to the kitchen, he heard Mario call after him. "Oh, and, kid, maybe you should cut back on the cartoons. I think they're putting a lot of weird ideas in that noggin of yours."

Billy looked around the kitchen for signs of the Hoove. Nothing. He opened the screen door and checked out the backyard. Nothing. He dashed to the oak tree and looked up into the top branches.

"If you're up there, get down here immediately," he called.

A squirrel poked his head out from behind a leaf.

"Not you," Billy said. "Unless you can read minds."

The Hoove was a no-show. There was only one thing left for Billy to do. He couldn't pretend to be getting a drink of water forever. He was going to have to go back to his room and tell

Ricardo and Ruby that the mind reading was off and the backward alphabet was on. They'd be very disappointed, that was for sure.

With a deep sigh, Billy went back inside and headed down the hall to his room. He was definitely not looking forward to the conversation.

CHAPTER 10

Billy pushed open the door of his room. Ricardo and Ruby were restlessly waiting for him.

"Dude, that was the longest drink of water in the history of drinks of water," Ricardo said. "I thought you were out there digging a well."

"I was preparing to tell you something really . . . well . . . let's just say . . . surprising," Billy answered, choosing his words very carefully.

"Do tell," boomed a ghostly voice. "Surprises water my melon."

Billy looked across the room and there, draped around the ceiling light fixture like a snake, was Hoover.

"Glad you could show up," Billy said to him.

"We've been here all along," Ricardo answered. "You're the one who went missing on us."

"I have to set the table in half an hour, so we

don't have much time," Ruby added. "I think we should get started."

She took out her purple glitter pen and spiral notebook.

"I'm going to take notes while Billy does his demonstration," she said. "I'll write down anything that needs improvement. Like if you say *um*. Mr. Wallwetter says that we have to eliminate all *um*s."

"*Um* . . . good idea," Ricardo said. They all cracked up. Even the Hoove let out a ghostly howl.

"Hey, Billy Boy," he cackled. "Your baseball friend is funny. The Hoove's Rule Number Three. Funny is good, which is also Rule Number Six Thirty-Three, Forty-Seven, and Fifty-Eight."

"Okay, Billy," Ruby said. "Start anytime."

It suddenly occurred to Billy that he wasn't sure what to get started on. He and the Hoove hadn't had time to discuss whose mind they were going to read and exactly what the trick was.

That's the trouble with a lie, he thought to himself. *It's just so easy for things to fall apart.*

"There are many ways to read a mind," he stalled. "It's hard to pick the best one."

Ruby and Ricardo were looking at him with great anticipation, but he had no idea how to do what he was supposed to do. He stood there frozen.

"Remain calm, Billy Boy," the Hoove said. "I am here to take charge in my usual take charge fashion. Now, send Ricardo into the closet."

"Ricardo," Billy said, pretending like he had just come up with a thought. "Can I ask you to step into my closet, please? Turn on the light and close the door behind you."

Ricardo was enjoying being part of the demonstration, so he gladly did as Billy said. Once inside the closet, he hollered out, "Okay, what's next?"

"Tell him to pick out three shirts and arrange them in any order he wants," the Hoove commanded.

Billy repeated the Hoove's instructions. He could hear the shuffling of hangers along the wooden bar in the closet.

"Got it," Ricardo shouted. "Can I come out now?"

"Remember the order, from right to left, that you put them in," Billy said. By then, he had figured out the Hoove's plan and he was able to take over the instructions.

"Done and done," Ricardo said, opening the closet door. Billy walked to the other side of the room and turned to face the wall, making it clear that he couldn't see into the closet.

"Ricardo, now I want you to sit down on the carpet," he commanded dramatically, "and let your mind focus on the three shirts. Clear all other thoughts away and send me the order you put them in. Do not say a word. Speak only with your mind."

"Way to go, Billy Boy. You're getting the knack of this thing," the Hoove said. "Now it's time for me to work my magic."

He floated across the room and shifted into his longest, thinnest shape, entering the closet through the keyhole.

"Ready when you are," he called from inside.

Billy placed his hands on his temples and closed his eyes.

"Okay, Ricardo. I will now tell you the order of the shirts, taking this information only from your mind. I'll need you to concentrate to the fullest."

"Listen carefully," the Hoove called from inside the closet. "From right to left, the first one up is . . . Hey, I thought I told you to throw this stupid shirt away. What part of throw away did you not understand?"

Billy could feel that Ricardo and Ruby were waiting eagerly for his answer. He rubbed his temples and pretended to be receiving a signal.

"Ricardo," he said. "You are not sending me a clear enough thought. Focus your mind and tell me which shirt is first. I repeat," he said, directing his voice toward the ghost in the closet, "*tell me which shirt is first!*"

"Okay, okay," the Hoove said, still muttering and fuming. "It's the one that says *I Fart . . . What's Your Superpower?* And this is the last time I'm telling you that you are much too cool a guy to be wearing fart joke shirts."

Billy made a mental note to take the shirt out of his closet and put it in his bottom drawer with his other favorite fart T-shirts. He would wear it when the Hoove was out.

"The first shirt up is the green one with the . . . *um . . . um . . .* okay, I'll just say it . . . fart joke. I'm so sorry, Ruby. I hope I didn't offend you."

"The only thing that bothered me was the two *ums*," Ruby said, scribbling furiously with her pencil. "Mr. Wallwetter says that *ums* are the enemy of pace."

"Who cares about *ums*?" Ricardo exclaimed. "Ruby, check out what this dude just did. He read my mind. That's incredible. Do it again. I'm going to focus on the other two."

"The next two shirts are your red and white baseball jersey and a button-down collared blue shirt that would actually look really good on me," the Hoove called.

Billy repeated what the Hoove told him, adding his own fanfare and sense of drama. All Ricardo could do was fall over on the rug in a stunned heap. Ruby put down her purple pen and stared at Billy.

"You're amazing," she said. Billy felt like he had just hit a home run in the World Series. He imagined the entire school standing in the auditorium Monday at the competition, clapping wildly and chanting his name. At last he would overcome his fear of public speaking. At last he would be a champion at something. At last he would be accepted. He wanted to jump up and down, but instead he just sauntered across the room, trying to give the impression that mind reading was something he did every day.

The Hoove slipped through the closet door out into the bedroom. He felt pretty great himself. He hoped the Higher-Ups had taken note of how much he was helping Billy.

Ricardo sniffed the air. "Do you smell something?" he asked. "Orange juice, maybe?"

"I don't smell anything." Billy shrugged. He had run out of made-up answers.

Ricardo and Ruby practiced their speeches next. Ricardo didn't have any carrots or raisins to make his salad, but he shredded notebook paper for the carrots and tossed in paper clips for the raisins. Halfway through Ruby's demonstration of her track warm-up techniques, the Hoove got bored and went out to the backyard to annoy the squirrels. He had a very short attention span.

"This was really a good rehearsal," Billy said as he walked Ruby and Ricardo to the front door. "Should we do another one tomorrow?"

"I can't," Ruby said. "It's Friday and we always have a team dinner on the last Friday of the month."

"I'll tell you what," Ricardo said to Billy. "Why don't you come to my house after school? We'll run through our speeches again and then maybe you can sleep over. I make a killer microwave pizza."

Billy couldn't believe what he was hearing. You didn't just ask anyone to sleep over and eat killer microwave pizza. You only asked your friends. Did that mean he and Ricardo were friends?

"You mean sleep over all night?" he asked.

"That's the way it usually works, dude. Unless you're a vampire."

"Sure," Billy said. "That'd be great. I mean, it sounds fun. I mean, totally fun."

Shut up, Billy, he said to himself. *You sound like such a dork.*

They walked down the driveway just as Bennett pulled up in a blue minivan.

"Hey, look, here comes my dentist," Ruby said. "Quick, Billy. Check my teeth to make sure there's no food stuck in them."

"You're good," said Billy after Ruby flashed him her uppers and lowers. He was amazed at Ruby's complete lack of embarrassment. He could have told her there was a fried chicken wing stuck between her two front teeth and it wouldn't have fazed her one bit. She was one confident person.

"Hi, kids!" Bennett waved as he walked up the driveway. "Ruby, I hope you're keeping up on your brushing. Don't forget the gums. A healthy gum is a happy gum."

"We were just practicing our speeches for the SOC competition on Monday," Billy said, trying to prevent Bennett from launching into a lecture on gum disease.

"I like your tie, Dr. Fielding," Ruby added.

Bennett Fielding was wearing a favorite from the large collection of tooth-oriented ties that he wore every day to the office. This one had a picture of a whole bunch of little teeth sitting on an ice cube. It said, YOU MAKE MY TEETH CHATTER.

"I hope Billy has decided to do the Floss-O-Rama," Bennett said. "I think it's a sure winner, don't you?"

Billy interrupted once again, before any more could be said about the virtues of putting string between your teeth.

"Bennett, Ricardo has asked me to sleep over tomorrow. Do you think that's okay?"

"Will your parents be home?" Dr. Fielding asked Ricardo.

"Are you kidding? The whole family's always there. I can't get rid of them."

"Well, then that sounds fine. Glad to see you boys are becoming friends. Hey, either of you two want a new toothbrush? I have a stash of them in the house."

"That's okay," Ruby said.

"Yeah, we have to get going," Ricardo added.

Billy felt incredibly happy as he waved Ruby and Ricardo good-bye. Even Bennett's embarrassing behavior couldn't ruin the moment. This new school thing was working out fine, just like his mom had promised. He was in such a good mood that when Breeze hollered at him to remove the fuzzy tomato from the bathroom counter, it didn't bother him. He just waved at her and hurried down the hall to his room. Hoover sat on the bed inside, tapping his foot impatiently.

"I thought those two would never leave," he said. "We have things to do."

"Like what?" Billy asked.

"I'm making great plans. I found some of Bennett's old golf clubs in the garage. I'm going to make a mini-golf course for us in the backyard that we can play when you get home from school tomorrow."

"Tomorrow?" Billy said. "As in Friday afternoon?"

"What? Do you have trouble with the days of the week? Yes, tomorrow. Friday. As in the day after Thursday. Or the day before Saturday. Take your pick."

"Uh, listen, Hoove," Billy began. "About tomorrow . . ."

"What about tomorrow? It's going to be great. Wait until you see the water hazard I'm building. It's going to blow you away. Fifty years of watching golf on TV finally paid off."

Billy wanted to tell the Hoove that he was busy, that he had made plans with Ricardo. But when he opened his mouth to tell him, the only thing that came out was, "Sounds great, Hoove. Can't wait."

Oh, well, Billy thought. *I'll tell him some other time. Like maybe never.*

CHAPTER 11

All the next day at school, Billy kept thinking about the sleepover at Ricardo's. He couldn't wait to see what kind of fun Ricardo had planned for them. Actually, it didn't even matter if Ricardo hadn't planned anything, if they twiddled their thumbs all night. The point was that he had been invited to sleep over at the house of not only a really nice guy, but the best player on the baseball team. And all because he was a mind reader.

Occasionally, as he sailed happily through his day, it occurred to Billy that he wasn't really a mind reader. That he had only passed himself off as one. But as soon as that thought popped into his head, he dismissed it. It got in the way of his newfound fame. When kids passed him in the hall and said hi, he answered with a confidence that surprised even him.

"Hey, Steve, how's it going, man?"

"Nice to see you, Zoe. Great scarf."

"Yo, Collin. Catch you in math."

It was the best day of school he could remember. He didn't worry about whether he was in the "in" group or the "out" group. He was able to just be Billy Broccoli and feel relaxed. It had never occurred to him before that it was possible for him to live in a worry-free zone.

As Billy closed his locker and headed for home, Ricardo handed him a note with directions to his house.

"It's only a couple blocks from you," he said. "Your parents won't even have to drop you off."

That was good news and bad news for Billy. The good news was that Ricardo lived close by so it'd be easy for them to hang out together a lot. The bad news was that Ricardo's house was within the Hoove's boundaries, and that meant he would have no trouble infiltrating the sleepover.

As he walked home, Billy rehearsed ways to tell the Hoove that he wasn't invited. He thought maybe using reverse psychology would work.

"Hoove," he'd say. "You are so beyond mortals like us that you would be bored stiff at a stupid little sleepover. I mean, nothing happens. We watch a little TV and eat a little popcorn. Big deal, you can't even digest it."

But as he crossed Moorepark and passed Patty's Coffee Shop, he realized that the reverse psychology angle wouldn't work on the Hoove. No way, no day. The Hoove was ready for any adventure, boring or not. So his next thought was to try flattery. Making Hoover feel important would work for sure.

"I need you to do me a favor," he'd say to the Hoove. "You know how Rod Brownstone noses around our property, and you're the only one who can put a stop to his annoying spy games? Could you please stay home and make sure he doesn't get up to anything sneaky? No one else is up to the task."

Billy decided that flattery was the best plan of attack. But when he finally got home and pushed open the door to his bedroom, his plan immediately fell apart. The Hoove was standing at the mirror, trying on his dress-up suspenders.

"Do you think these are too formal for the sleepover?" he asked. "Because I don't want to embarrass anybody by overdressing. For my casual look, I've already packed your baseball jersey, which I knew you'd let me borrow because you're that kind of generous guy."

Billy gulped.

"How'd you know about the sleepover?"

"I heard Bennett telling your mom. These ears are not only good-looking, they also have a keen sense of hearing."

"So, about the sleepover, Hoove," Billy stammered. "I have several thoughts I want to discuss with you."

"Put those thoughts away," the Hoove called over his shoulder as he tossed one of Billy's baseballs into Billy's overnight bag. "Because we're heading for a great time. I see a catch in our future. Not to mention ghost stories before bed . . . of which I have more than a few. They will amaze and thrill the gathering. I can see us now, sitting around the campfire."

"Hoove, we're not allowed to make fires. We're kids."

"Billy Boy, you are a dream crusher. But I'm going to let that slide tonight because I am in such a great mood about the sleepover. As a matter of fact — drumroll please — this is my first sleepover in ninety-nine years."

Billy's mouth opened and not a sound came out. All the plans he had made walking home were caught in his throat. He had just screwed up the courage to tell the Hoove he couldn't go, and now, listening to his excitement, Billy's courage evaporated like water on a summer sidewalk. He didn't have the heart to say no.

"Listen, Hoove, you've got to promise me something," he said firmly.

The Hoove zipped up Billy's overnight bag and turned to face Billy, a big smile on his handsome face.

"My ears are at attention."

"No kidding. I really need you to listen to me and keep your word."

"Okay. Will you spill the beans already?"

"Ricardo doesn't know about you, and he's not going to. He's a brand-new friend, and he doesn't need to know I have a personal ghost. Nobody does, for that matter."

"Are you embarrassed by me?"

"In a word, yes. He'll think I'm nutso if I tell him about you. So here are a few of Billy's rules for you. No floating popcorn when we're watching TV. Actually, no floating popcorn ever. No howling or creaking sounds. No baseballs whizzing around the room on their own. No wedgies when we're asleep."

"Now you've gone too far! What's a sleepover without a wedgie?"

"Hoove, what I'm saying is that you have to be invisible."

"What are you talking about? In case you haven't noticed, I am invisible."

"Good. Stay that way. That's all I'm asking."

Billy felt a vibration in his pocket and reached for his cell phone. It was a text from Ricardo. It said:

Get here now. I have a big surprise.

Throwing the last of his things into his backpack, Billy headed down the hall toward the back door. The Hoove followed behind, quiet as a mouse.

Breeze was in the kitchen making a grilled cheese sandwich that smelled so delicious, Billy's nose practically did a backflip.

"Want one?" she asked as Billy came into the kitchen.

"No time," he said. "But it sure smells great. Tell Mom that I left for Ricardo's. I'll call her when I get there."

"Wow, look who's developed a major social life," Breeze commented. "Not bad for a career nerd."

Billy didn't even bother to answer. He was out the door before she'd even finished her sentence. The Hoove, however, couldn't resist picking up the pepper shaker when her back was turned and covering the top of her sandwich with a spicy layer of pepper. That would teach her to insult his pal.

Ricardo lived about three blocks away, on Babcock Lane. In the Hoove's day, the block had sat on the edge of the family ranchero property, out behind the avocado and orange groves. Back then, it was a flat, grass-covered pasture that they'd used for grazing cattle. Over the years, the cattle had been replaced by three-bedroom homes with a herd of minivans, one parked in each driveway.

As Billy turned the corner onto Babcock

Lane, the Hoove dipping and diving through the air behind him, he saw Ricardo waiting on his front lawn. Standing next to him was an older man wearing a blue satin Dodgers zip-up jacket.

"You must be Mr. Perez," Billy said as he approached the man, extending his hand to shake as his mother had always taught him to do. "Nice to meet you, sir."

"Tell him he's got a cool jacket," the Hoove whispered in Billy's ear. "That will impress him."

"You're right, man. This is Mr. Perez," Ricardo said, "but he's not my father. He's my father's older brother, my Uncle Tito."

"Nice to meet you, too, Mr. Also Perez," Billy answered. The man laughed a huge hearty laugh at Billy's little joke. Billy liked him right away, but he liked him even better when Uncle Tito told him the exciting news.

"How would you like to go on a private tour of Dodger Stadium?" he asked. "That includes the dugout, the locker room, the batting cage, and the announcer's box."

Billy looked at Ricardo. "He's kidding, right?"

Ricardo shook his head.

"Maybe I could even let you run the bases on

the field and stand in the on-deck circle," Uncle Tito added. "Just don't ask to throw a ball from the pitcher's mound. That's sacred ground."

Billy's jaw dropped about a mile. He assumed this was all a big joke, but Uncle Tito wasn't laughing.

"My uncle is one of the groundskeepers at Dodger Stadium," Ricardo explained. "He's arranged to show us around tonight."

"Amazing" was all Billy could say.

"Yeah, it's pretty cool," Ricardo said. "He's taken me once before, but tonight he said I could bring a guest."

"Thank you a million billion trillion gazillion babillion times," Billy said to Mr. Perez, grabbing his hand and shaking it like a water pump. "This could be the best night of my entire life. No. Wait a minute. It *is* the best night of my entire life."

Uncle Tito laughed that big hearty laugh of his.

"I understand your excitement," he said. "I've been working at Dodger Stadium for ten years, and every time I walk in there, I feel the magic like it was the first time."

"When do we leave?" Billy said. He was so excited that he didn't notice the Hoove stomping back and forth across the lawn like a two-year-old throwing a tantrum.

"How about now?" Uncle Tito suggested.

"Now is not soon enough," Billy answered, and Uncle Tito laughed again.

"You got a funny friend," he said to Ricardo. "I'll go get my truck from down the street. Ricardo, go grab the sandwiches your mom made. They're in the kitchen. Billy, you wait here and we'll be right back."

As Uncle Tito walked toward his truck and Ricardo headed into the house, the Hoove flew into Billy's face and took off into the rant of the century.

"Tell me this isn't happening," he howled. "You're just going to leave me here? You know I can't go to Dodger Stadium. It's way beyond my boundaries."

"What do you want me to do, Hoove? I didn't know this was going to happen."

"You didn't know? Well, I'll tell you what you know. You know that it's my dream, my all-time, most important, deep-seated, biggest-ever dream to see the baseball stadiums of America. I know you know that!"

Billy nodded. The Hoove had told him that many times.

"So how can you go to one of those stadiums without me? Tell me how that's fair?"

"It isn't, Hoove. But what do you want me to do? Not go?"

"Yes. That's exactly what I want. I mean no, that's not what I want. I mean yes. I mean no. I mean . . . I don't know."

"Well, that clears things up."

"All I know, my ex-buddy, is that this is the worst. My dream is so close, it's right there under my well-chiseled nose, and yet it's so far. And you're going to live it instead of me."

Billy was quiet for a moment. He heard the sadness in the Hoove's voice, and he didn't know what to say or do.

"I can take pictures for you on my cell phone," he suggested meekly. "I'll capture every detail, I promise."

"Pictures?" The Hoove was shouting now. "I've seen Dodger Stadium on television. I've seen it in magazines. I don't need a picture. I need to *be there* in person. To smell the grass. To feel the dirt under my feet."

Billy had never heard that tone of voice come from the Hoove. Whether he was angry or bored or impatient or frustrated, he was always so full of attitude. Like the coolest actor playing his part. But standing there on the lawn of Ricardo's house, the Hoove's attitude melted away, and he sounded just like any other kid whose heart was breaking with disappointment. Billy reached out to place a comforting hand on Hoover's shoulder.

"Hey, man, what's with the arm in the air?" Ricardo said, surprising Billy as he came bouncing down the front steps of the house, holding a wicker picnic basket. Realizing that he must look like an idiot, Billy pulled his hand back fast.

"I appreciate the gesture," the Hoove said, "even if it was short-lived. But what I'd appreciate more is if you told Mr. Baseball here that you suddenly got called home."

Ricardo was heading to the curb, where Uncle Tito had just pulled up in his blue Ford truck.

"What excuse could I give him?" Billy asked the Hoove.

"Tell him that your best friend needs you."

"Come on, Billy!" Ricardo called. "We can't keep our private tour waiting."

Billy watched Ricardo climb into the front seat of the truck. Uncle Tito honked the horn and beckoned him.

"Dodger Express," he called out. "All aboard."

Billy stood there on the lawn. His feet felt like cement blocks. It was as if he were divided in two. Everything on his right side was telling him to go get in the truck and have a great time. Everything on his left side was telling him to stay with the Hoove.

Right side.

Left side.

Right side.

Left side.

What was a guy to do?

CHAPTER 12

The Hoove couldn't believe his eyes as he watched Billy walk away from him, climb into the truck, and close the door. His heart practically broke when he saw the truck pull away from the curb and head down the street, block after block, until it was just a tiny blue speck disappearing on the horizon.

After all I've done for that kid, he thought, *this is the thanks I get. He's off to Dodger Stadium and I'm standing here on the lawn like a pink plastic flamingo stuck in the grass.*

The Hoove's sadness turned to rage. Even though he knew nobody could hear him, he started to shout.

"All right. You know what? I've had it. I quit. I'm turning in my ghost badge. You hear that, Higher-Ups? You win. Take my report card and shred it. See if I care. Oh, and let me answer that for you . . . I don't!"

He waited for a response, any response. A flash of lightning, a crow flying, a rock exploding in flames. But all he got was silence.

"Okay, don't answer me," he shouted into the emptiness. "I don't need your advice anyway. Hoover Porterhouse the Third has always been on his own, and will remain so. Thank you and good-bye."

He flipped into hyperglide and took off down the street for whereabouts unknown. He flew by Mrs. Pearson, who was climbing off her electric lawn mower after a good mow. It was not easy for her to dismount since each of her thighs was the size of a Thanksgiving turkey. Normally, the Hoove might have stopped to help her, giving her leg an invisible lift. But he was in such an emotional tizzy that he could think of nothing but himself and his own anger.

As usual in times of crisis, he found himself heading to the baseball diamond in Live Oak Park. Even though he couldn't actually walk onto the field, it made him feel better just to be close to it. He pulled to a stop at the left field fence and perched on top of it, hanging his legs over the chain link, but being careful that they never touched the ground.

Out of the corner of his eye, the Hoove noticed a wiggling bank of fog appear on the pitcher's mound. As it moved closer and closer to him, he saw that it was the distinctive figure of Yogi Berra walking toward him again. Although he wore a Yankees cap on his head, he wasn't wearing his uniform. Instead, he had on a floral bathing suit and an unbuttoned matching Hawaiian shirt. His knees were covered in thick white sunscreen.

"Not you again," the Hoove said.

"Oh yes, kiddo. Me again," Yogi answered. "And I'm not exactly thrilled to be here, either. Ten seconds ago, I was sitting on the beach in Miami spreading suntan lotion around my knee area and lolling around in my swimming trunks."

"Oh, is that what you call that tropical garden adorning your body?"

"Can you explain something to me, kiddo? Why are you always in such a foul mood?"

"I have every right to be. You know what good old Billy Broccoli just did? Took off and left me in the dust. The kid goes to Dodger Stadium, which happens to be my ninety-nine-year dream, but do I get to go? No, he does. Tell me how that's fair. I have been thinking about visiting baseball stadiums longer than he's been alive."

"Yeah, everyone knows that."

"Wait a minute," the Hoove said, eyeing Yogi suspiciously. "Are you sure you're not one of the Higher-Ups?"

"I already told you I'm not. I'm just a messenger. I hear things through the grapevine."

"Oh really? Because you seem to know everything about me, which makes me think that either you're one of them or you get a paycheck from them."

"You got a lot of mouth, kiddo, but not much to back it up."

"Listen to me, Yogi. First of all, I think you should change your name. You sound like a frog. And second of all, I quit. I'm done with the ghost business. It's busting me in half. I mean, who does that kid think he is? He is nothing without me. Zero. Wait a minute, let's ponder this. What is less than zero?"

"Beats me, kid. The only math I know is batting averages."

"All right, I'll tell you what it is. Minus zero. Billy Broccoli is a minus zero without me. I do everything for him. Pick his clothes. Show him how to walk without grinning like a two-year-old that just filled up his diapers. I'm working nonstop to put some swagger in his life. And he goes off to live my dream without a second thought."

"So you're going to quit, just like that? And be confined to this small suburban neighborhood for all eternity? I'd think twice about that, kid. It'd feel mighty awful."

"How do you know how I feel?" The Hoove was shouting now. "You get to go to steak restaurants and sit on the beach and travel across the country whenever they call you. I'm stuck on this one little ranchero in Southern California. And the only way I can get out is by helping a kid who refuses to take the sweet nuggets of advice that I drop in his lap like candy."

"That's not what's eating you," Yogi said. "You're jealous because Broccoli got to go to Dodger Stadium and you were left behind. That hurt you. I understand that."

"What are you, the world authority on emotions?"

"That's exactly what I am. A manager has to know each player's personality and figure out what's going on in his messed-up head. You keep taking your eye off the ball. The goal here is to help Billy move on. That's the only way you're going to help yourself move on and realize your own dreams. And you can't stick to the plan."

"Easier said than done."

"It's not all that complicated, kid. Nothing comes for free in this world. The energy you put in is the energy you get back."

"That sounds like something my grandma Gertrude embroidered on a pillow."

"Good for her. She knew something you haven't learned yet. See, you're thinking about giving up on Billy, but what you're really doing is giving up on yourself. That's what people do when they're afraid."

"Oh really? And what exactly am I afraid of? Let me answer that for you. Nothing."

"You don't fool me, Mr. Ghost with an Attitude. You're afraid that you're never going to get to all those stadiums you dream about because you don't believe you've got the stuff to help Billy be the best he can be. So you figure that giving up is easier than failing."

Hoover Porterhouse was silent for a long minute, and Yogi saw that his point had finally hit home.

"Giving up is not the only way, Hoover," he said quietly. "You're at a fork in the road. And I say, when you come to a fork in the road, take it."

Before Hoover could ask what that meant, Yogi took a few steps back and began to disappear into the fog.

"So now you're going, just like that?" Hoover shouted after him. "Fine. And in case you haven't noticed, you're leaving globs of suntan lotion all over the infield."

"Remember what I said, kiddo." Yogi's voice echoed across center field as his body disappeared into the swirl of fog. "It ain't over 'til it's over."

"Thanks for the tip," the Hoove shouted into the distance. "Maybe someday I'll figure out what that means."

The Hoove sat in the darkness, not moving from the chain-link fence. He didn't feel like flying or floating or gliding. He didn't feel like cruising around looking for fun. He just felt like thinking. And thinking was something he was not at all accustomed to.

CHAPTER 13

The next morning, Billy burst into his bedroom full of enthusiasm. He couldn't wait to tell the Hoove all about his trip to Dodger Stadium. He had taken about a hundred pictures with his cell phone, and had even brought the Hoove a surprise souvenir that almost no one else in the world could possibly have.

"Hey, Hoove!" he called out. "Where are you? Make yourself visible. Come on. I want to hear you whistle 'I've Been Working on the Railroad.'"

But instead of whistling, he heard only silence.

"Okay," Billy said, picking up the corner of his bedspread and glancing under it. "I get it. You're still mad that I had to leave you behind. Who wouldn't be? But you're not going to be mad anymore when you see what I've got for you. I promise."

More silence.

"So you're playing hard to get," Billy said with a knowing smile. "No problem. If you won't come to me, I'll come to you."

Billy tiptoed over to the closet and flung open the door. He sniffed for the aroma of fresh oranges, but all he smelled was the gym shoes that he had forgotten to leave on the porch to air out.

"So Mr. Porterhouse is hiding," he said, closing the closet door. "Hmmm, I wonder where a ghost would hide in my room."

Billy crept over to his chest of drawers, bent down quietly, then with a sudden motion, pulled the bottom drawer open.

"Gotcha!"

But the Hoove was not inside. In fact, the only things in that drawer were his three hooded sweatshirts and a whole lot of mismatched socks. From his crouched position, Billy glanced around the room, checking under the bed and behind the desk. Still nothing. He got up and went to the window. Pressing his face against the glass, he looked for the Hoove, expecting to see him hovering outside Rod

Brownstone's house with a prank in mind. But no one was there.

"Please don't tell me you're licking the glass clean?" came Breeze's voice from the doorway. "They have products for that, you know."

Breeze had busted in without knocking, as usual. They had only been brother and sister for less than a month, but Billy had already learned that the word *privacy* was not in her vocabulary.

"Listen, Breeze," Billy said. "You didn't happen to smell orange juice going down the hall or in your room, did you?"

"You know what, Billy? If I didn't need a favor from you, I would nail a sign to your door that says BEWARE! CRAZY DUDE INSIDE, and run away screaming. However, I need to borrow your iPod charger, so I'm not at liberty to do that. Oh, look, there it is."

She grabbed Billy's charger from the nightstand next to his bed.

"I'll return it as soon as I can. And in the meantime, keep your tongue off the glass. It leaves streaks."

Billy could hear her laughing as she padded back down the hall to her room. She certainly got a kick out of herself, which was a quality Billy admired and resented at the same time.

The Hoove must be out in his oak tree, Billy thought. *It's the place he goes when he's upset.*

Billy hurried down the hall into the kitchen. He was hoping his mom and stepdad weren't there so he could head right into the backyard without pausing to tell them all about the sleepover. He wanted to apologize to the Hoove because he truly did feel bad that his friend had missed out on going to Dodger Stadium. But before he could get out the back door, he ran smack into his mother and Bennett sitting at the kitchen table.

"Good morning, sweetie," his mom chirped. "Tell us all about the sleepover."

"I can't now, Mom. I got stuff to do in the backyard."

"Maybe I'll join you, Bill," Bennett said. "Have a little man-to-man time. I'll show you the new sprinkler system I'm installing. I went for the brass valves. Nothing plastic for me. No, sir, I don't believe in skimping on sprinklers."

"Bennett, you have such an eye for quality products," Billy's mom said.

"Wait until I tell you about the new drill I ordered for the office. It's vibration free."

"Your patients are lucky to have such an innovative dentist," Mrs. Broccoli-Fielding commented, taking her new husband's hand. That was all the encouragement Bennett needed to launch into a long-winded description of dental drills, with more details than anyone would ever want to hear in a lifetime. Billy didn't mind, though, because Bennett's lecture gave him the opportunity to slip out the back door unnoticed and run over to Hoover's tree.

He stood at the base and looked up, but there was no Hoove in sight. That didn't mean he wasn't there — it just meant he wasn't *visible*. Billy started to whistle "I've Been Working on the Railroad." He figured if the Hoove was there, he'd join in and then poof, he'd materialize. He got through the whole song, all the way up to "Someone's in the kitchen with Dinah," and still he didn't hear even the tiniest whistle from the Hoove.

Suddenly, he heard leaves rustling from the top branches.

"Hoove? Is that you? Please let that be you."

Another rustle.

"Don't be cute, man. Listen, I'm sorry about everything. I shouldn't have ditched you. I didn't know how to say no to Ricardo because he's just starting to be my friend. Let's forget it and get back to normal. We have work to do before Monday."

Another rustle. Billy's eyes followed the sound until he noticed a bushy-tailed squirrel darting from branch to branch. His heart sank.

"I don't suppose you can shape-shift into a squirrel," Billy called out. "But if you could, I would say to you that I'm really sorry. And if you don't forgive me, I understand. I wouldn't want to be treated the way I treated you."

The squirrel stopped, stared at him inquisitively, and then tossed a rotting acorn at his head.

"Okay, I deserve that," Billy called out. "And I just want to say one more thing. You're my friend, and not just because of the SOC competition. I like hanging out with you."

The squirrel twitched his nose and cocked his head, then jumped onto a telephone wire and scampered off to Mrs. Pearson's yard.

"Wow, I can't believe I just had a conversation with a squirrel."

Billy turned to walk back into the house, never knowing that Hoover had been in the tree the whole time, hanging on the branch above the squirrel and hearing every word Billy had said. He could have made himself visible, but his anger won out over his ability to forgive. What the Hoove couldn't have known was that the Higher-Ups were watching him the whole time, jotting down notes in their gigantic parchment ledger about his need to learn forgiveness.

For the rest of the day, Billy waited for the Hoove to show up. He couldn't concentrate on anything. He tried playing video games, doing homework, and making grilled cheese sandwiches with tomato slices. He even tried matching up the socks in his bottom drawer.

Nothing could distract him from the fact that Hoover had left him.

Sunday came and went without the appearance of any ghostly signs. Before dinner, Billy got a call from Ruby.

"You all set for tomorrow?" she asked.

"No problem," he answered. "I'm throwing my mind-reading vibes into high gear. I can feel the win already."

Of course, that was all a lie. The call made Billy even more frantic. The SOC competition was only sixteen hours away. He couldn't believe that the Hoove would abandon him now without even giving him a chance to apologize. Was he really that selfish? Had Billy hurt his feelings that much or was the Hoove just being his usual irresponsible self?

By the time the family sat down to Sunday night family dinner, Billy was beside himself with anxiety. He didn't have a backup plan. Without the Hoove's participation in the mind-reading stunt, he was going to let Ruby and Ricardo down with a thud, not to mention embarrass himself beyond repair.

"Here's your plate, just the way you like it," Mrs. Broccoli-Fielding said to Billy, putting down a heaping serving of scrambled eggs and fresh, crispy bacon.

Billy and his mom had a Sunday night dinner tradition. Ever since he was little, she made breakfast for dinner — bacon and sausages and scrambled eggs and sometimes even French toast with cinnamon and sugar. When they moved in with Bennett and Breeze, Mrs. Broccoli-Fielding suggested they continue the tradition.

"Pass the ketchup, please," Billy said morosely. Even breakfast for dinner couldn't cheer him up.

Billy's mom slid the ketchup bottle closer to his plate before she went back to the stove to make Breeze's plate.

"Breeze, tell me again if you like soft scrambled eggs or the more well-done ones," she said, examining the remaining eggs in the skillet. "There are plenty of both."

"Definitely well-done," Breeze answered. "The runny part makes me gag. And speaking of gagging, can I ask you, Billy, what are you thinking? Seriously?"

Billy looked at her blankly. "What's the problem?"

"You're drowning your scrambled eggs in ketchup. Who eats like that?"

"I do."

"Has anyone ever told you it's gross?"

"No."

"Well, then, let me be the first. It's stomach-churningly gross."

"Breeze, let Billy enjoy his meal the way he likes it," Bennett said. "Dinner isn't a time for us to judge one another. It's a time to share. Now who wants to go first and tell us what you're looking forward to in the coming week?"

There was no response from Billy or Breeze.

"Why don't you start, Bennett?" Billy's mom suggested as she brought the last two plates to the table and slid into her chair.

"Don't mind if I do. I have a lot to look forward to this week — two root canals on Tuesday. And on Wednesday, I'm putting a gold filling in Mr. Schneider's back molar. It will be a real challenge to get my drill bit back there, but I always enjoy a good a dental challenge."

"Dad, that's almost as repulsive as Billy's red eggs," Breeze commented.

"Fine, Breeze. Then you go next. What are you looking forward to this week?"

"The Dark Cloud plays its first concert this coming Friday afternoon. We're going to rock the house."

"That's if you call playing for the chess club a concert," Billy said, his mouth full of bacon.

"I do. Besides, what do you have this week that's any better?"

"Oh, Billy has something very, very exciting happening tomorrow," Mrs. Broccoli-Fielding said. "Tell them, Billy."

Billy stopped mid-chew and felt his stomach do a backflip. He had momentarily put the SOC competition out of his mind so that he could enjoy the crunch of his bacon.

"It's no big deal, Mom."

"Why yes it is. Tomorrow, Billy is representing Mr. Wallwetter's class in the SOC competition." Billy could tell that his mom was really proud of him. He didn't usually get singled out for special honors.

Billy's appetite had completely vanished. His mother's words, meant to make him feel good, had actually had the opposite effect. Bennett reached out, picked up his glass of orange juice, and held it in the air.

"I'd like to propose a toast," he said. "To Billy. May the words flow from your mouth like the water from my dental hose."

The family clinked their glasses. Everyone except Billy. He couldn't join in the toast. He was too busy thinking that he *was* toast!

CHAPTER 14

Monday morning came all too soon. And there was still no sign of the Hoove.

Billy was a bundle of nerves. He hung over the sink in the boys' bathroom, splashing cold water on his face. As he pulled a paper towel from the dispenser and patted his face dry, he checked the clock on the wall. Ten minutes to ten. He was supposed to be in the auditorium, helping Ruby and Ricardo make their name tags and set up their chairs on the stage, but he had excused himself to go to the bathroom for the fourth time in the last half hour.

"Man, you must have had a lot of liquids at breakfast," Ricardo had commented.

"You can't be too careful when you have to appear in public," Billy answered. "You don't want any lakes appearing where there shouldn't be lakes . . . if you catch my drift."

"Can I just say I don't and leave it at that?"

Billy instantly wished he hadn't said what he said. Of course, Ricardo didn't want to discuss his peeing situation. No one would. But what else could he have said to explain his behavior? That his personal ghost — the one who was responsible for his mind-reading trick — was a no-show? That he had nothing ready to take its place? That he was going to let his team down in front of the whole school? No, making repeated trips to the bathroom seemed a much better solution.

Billy's heart raced as he stood at the sink visualizing the auditorium filling with all four hundred of Moorepark's students. He imagined the team from Ms. Winter's sixth-grade class setting up their chairs on the opposite side of the stage. He saw the three teachers acting as judges checking the sound system, and Mr. Wallwetter pacing back and forth, his skinny mustache soaking wet with anxious perspiration.

All Billy could do was blot his T-shirt with paper towels to clean up the water that had missed his face. He knew there was no turning back. He was just going to have to go out there and face the consequences, whatever they were. He turned off the water and breathed deeply. Suddenly, the pipes rumbled as if something was stuck inside.

Oh, great, Billy thought. *As if this day isn't bad enough, now I'm going to be the center of a plumbing emergency.*

The pipes continued to vibrate, growing louder and louder until it seemed like the sink was going to break loose from the wall. Billy fidgeted with the cold faucet, trying desperately to get the noise to stop. It was then he heard it — a distant whistling that seemed to be coming from inside the spout.

No, it couldn't be.

But it was.

As Billy stared at the faucet, a plaid newsboy cap with a button on top emerged from the spout, streaming out like liquid smoke. After the cap came a face. After the face came suspenders, and after the suspenders came brown leather boots laced up to the ankle. Finally, an entire Hoover Porterhouse III oozed out of the faucet and stood upright in the sink, a moist smile plastered on his face.

"I am here," he said, snapping his suspenders with a cocky grin.

"You came through the pipes?"

"That I did, and I might add, with extreme flair. The Hoove's Rule Number Fifty-Five. Seize the room and command the crowd with your entrance."

"Hoove, no one's here. It's just you and me . . . and the toilet."

"Billy Boy, there are no small rooms, only small entrances."

The Hoove jumped out of the sink and checked himself out in the mirror, slicking back his handsome head of hair. He was all smiles, acting like nothing was wrong. His casual attitude made Billy furious.

"I can't believe you just vanished on me," Billy snapped. "I've been so worried I haven't been able to sleep or eat, except for last night when my appetite came back a little because the bacon was really good."

"Understood. I've always loved a good strip of bacon myself."

"Listen, Hoove, I'm sorry about going to Dodger Stadium without you, but you didn't have to go disappear on me. I've been a nervous wreck. Where have you been?"

"Never mind where *I've* been," the Hoove said, laying a cold hand on Billy's shoulder. "Calm yourself down, my friend, and think about where *you're* going. Out on that stage to wow them."

"I can't wow anyone. We haven't rehearsed. We don't even know if the mind-reading thing is going to work again."

"Get serious, Billy Boy. Do I look like an entity that ever rehearsed in his life? I'm a natural at the supernatural."

There was a knock on the bathroom door, and Ricardo stuck his head in.

"Hey, dude, you all right in here?" he asked. "I thought I heard conversation."

"Um ... I was just rehearsing," Billy said. "I'm fine, Ricardo. I just need another few minutes to go over my stuff."

"I can't give 'em to you," Ricardo said. "Wallwetter told me to come get you right away. Let's go."

"As in now?"

"Why, you got other plans?"

"Tell him we're ready," the Hoove told Billy. "Go ahead. Look confident."

"I'm . . . I'm . . . I'm ready," Billy stammered.

"Excuse me," the Hoove interrupted. "I believe I said *we're* ready!"

Ricardo was already out the door. Checking himself in the mirror one last time, Billy smoothed his lumpy hair as best he could and followed Ricardo out into the hall. The Hoove was right behind him.

As they approached the auditorium, Billy thought he heard a hive of buzzing bees inside. The entire sixth, seventh, and eighth grades were talking and laughing and waiting rest-lessly for the competition to start. Billy walked down the aisle and up the wooden stairs onto the stage. Ruby was already seated, her name tag hanging around her neck. Ricardo sat down next to her, and Billy took the remaining seat. Ms. Winter's team was busily going over their notes on the other side of the stage. The Hoove floated to the center and took a deep bow.

"Too bad you guys can't see me," he called out to the audience, "because I'm about to per-form the perfect moonwalk."

In his day, the Hoove had been a terrific dancer, and during his time as a ghost, he had learned all the popular dances of the last hundred years. He could do the Charleston, the jitterbug, the tango, the twist, the mashed potato, and even the funky chicken. What he loved best was the moonwalk. When he did it, it seemed like he was floating on air (which technically he was). As he began his perfect moonwalk across the stage, the Hoove shot a glance over at Billy.

"I know what you're thinking," he said. "That old Hoover Porterhouse can bust a move."

And with that, he moonwalked down the stairs and up the aisle, coming to a stop next to the seat occupied by Rod Brownstone. Just for fun, he blew in Brownstone's right ear. Rod promptly turned to Spencer Robinson, a muscular eighth grader who was sitting to the right of him, and slugged him in the arm.

"What'd you do that for?" Spencer snapped, pulling himself up to his full height. "Actually, Brownstone, I don't care what you did it for. If you do it again, I'm going to paper clip your lips together."

Rod backed off right away, flashing Spencer a timid grin and dropping the subject immediately. Like all bullies, Brownstone was a coward at heart and as soon as he was challenged, he sunk down into the cushion of his auditorium seat.

Mr. Wallwetter tapped on the microphone to get the assembly's attention and began the introduction of his team. As he spoke, the Hoove floated around the auditorium looking for the person whose mind he was going to read. After much consideration, he settled on Tess Wu, who was texting from a phone hidden in the folds of her purse so that the teachers couldn't see it. The Hoove looked over her shoulder and saw that she was telling Ava Daley about a new pair of purple and silver running shoes she was going to buy that day.

"This will work nicely," he shouted out to Billy. "When I give you the signal, you tell them she's thinking about buying purple and silver running shoes. I'll give you more details as I get them."

By that time, Mr. Wallwetter had finished his introductions. Ms. Winter took the microphone to introduce her team, which consisted of Emily Yamaguchi, Samir Shah, and Paul Costello. Ms. Winter announced that Emily would demonstrate how to make an origami bird out of a dollar bill. Samir would demonstrate how to bend a stream of water using static electricity. And the final presentation would be Paul Costello demonstrating his wheelchair basketball skills.

"We've got some stiff competition," Ruby whispered.

"No worries," Ricardo said, throwing an arm around Billy. "We got the B Bomb here. No one's going to beat him."

Billy silently thanked his lucky stars that the Hoove had shown up in time. Without him, the B Bomb would have fizzled out like a two-week-old can of soda. Billy looked nervously into the audience and was relieved to see the Hoove busily checking out Tess's phone messages. She was watching the stage and didn't notice her phone drifting slightly above her purse.

"Getting all the goods on her," the Hoover called out. "Trust me, we are going to amaze and delight. This trophy is in the bag . . . of that you can be sure."

The teachers flipped a coin to determine which team would go first, and Ms. Winter's team won. Emily Yamaguchi and her origami dollar bill bird were up first. She did a good demonstration of something that was obviously hard to do. After she finished, the three judges each held up a paddle with a number from one to ten. Emily got all sevens. The judges said that they had to take points off because she said *um* and *like* too much.

Ruby went next, and although she was extremely flexible while demonstrating her warm-up exercises, she completely toppled over during one of her lunges. She wasn't hurt, and after taking a few seconds to collect herself, she stood back up and finished her routine. The judges gave her two eights and a nine. The eights were because she had fallen and the nine was for having the poise to get back up and finish her routine.

When Ruby took her seat, Billy and Ricardo gave her high fives.

"At least I got us in the lead." She shrugged. "Even if I did lunge sideways." Then, in typical Ruby fashion, she laughed. Billy was in awe of her self-confidence, that she could fall over in front of everyone and not be even the slightest bit embarrassed. He wondered if he would ever believe in himself that much.

Next, Samir and Ricardo went head-to-head. Samir spoke first and demonstrated how the static electricity from a balloon that had been rubbed on a sweater could bend a stream of water. But his experiment didn't work because he rubbed the balloon too hard and it popped before he could hold it up to the water. Luckily, he had a plastic comb in his pocket, and when he rubbed that on his sweater, it did the trick. The trickle of water bent toward the comb. Unluckily, Samir had forgotten to clean the hair out of his plastic comb, and when he was finished with the experiment, his white sweater had some serious strands of black hair traveling down the front. He got two eights and one seven from the judges. Two of the judges felt that he knew his science, but he didn't project his voice to the back of the room. The third judge didn't explain her score of seven, but chances were she objected to the hair party on his sweater.

Ricardo had a strong start to his carrot and raisin salad demonstration. Unfortunately, he got some points taken off for dropping a clump of mayonnaise on the floor and then cracking up about it. When Ricardo started to laugh onstage, Billy glanced over at Mr. Wallwetter in the wings and could practically see smoke coming out of his ears. He was fuming.

"Maintain your composure," he hissed at Ricardo. "There is nothing funny about spilled mayonnaise."

Ricardo managed to finish his speech without cracking up again, but his eyes kept watering the way they do when you're trying to stifle a laugh. He scored two sevens and a nine. To no one's surprise, the nine was from Coach Johnston of the baseball team, who may have been a little biased in favor of his best home-run hitter. That made Ricardo's score twenty-three, the same as Samir's. Mr. Wallwetter's team was four points in the lead.

Ms. Winter announced that since the score was close, the winner of the competition was probably going to be determined by the last two contestants — Paul Costello and Billy Broccoli.

She was looking forward to seeing how these two contestants would perform under such pressure.

Paul Costello went first. Billy hadn't met him yet, because they didn't have any classes together, but he knew that Paul was a friend of Breeze's. All Breeze had told him was that Paul was a really nice guy and that he had been in a wheelchair most of his life because of a lower spinal cord injury.

Paul rolled his chair up to the microphone and asked Ms. Winter to take it away. Then he took a headset from his lap and slid it around his head. It had a thin wire microphone that led to his mouth, allowing him to speak and be heard without using his hands.

"A lot of you might think that people in wheelchairs are limited," he said to the kids in the auditorium. "I'm here to demonstrate that our limits are only in our mind. I've always wanted to play basketball, and I wasn't going to let this chair stop me. So please watch and enjoy as I demonstrate wheelchair basketball skills."

Billy could feel the crowd moving to the edge of their seats. Even Ricardo leaned forward, eager to see what Paul could do.

"I'll start off with basic wheelchair movements such as the forward and backward push, the turn, the pivot, and the tilt," Paul began. "Then I'll show you a bounce pass and a chest pass. And I'll end with a few different dribbles I've perfected over the years."

What followed was a dazzling display of athletic prowess. Paul moved his wheelchair up and down the stage with lightning speed. It was like it had a motor, only the motor was his two hands on the wheels. He moved with such grace and hustle that the audience almost forgot he was confined to a chair. As he pivoted and tilted, he explained how he used his hands and his torso to propel himself and maintain his balance.

The passing demonstration was equally impressive. Billy watched in amazement as Paul shot chest passes and bounce passes across the stage to Samir and Emily. All Billy could think was that Paul was a better athlete with half his body than Billy was with his whole one. Ricardo leaned over and whispered in his ear.

"You better do a humongous job, dude, because this guy rocks."

What Ricardo didn't know was that Paul hadn't even gotten to the good part yet. His dribbling demonstration was so dramatic that you could actually hear people in the audience gasping in amazement. Before he started, Samir and Emily set up orange cones in a straight line along the stage. Then Paul set off in his wheelchair, dribbling the ball and weaving between the cones until he reached the other side. On the way back, he did the same thing . . . dribbling two balls!

The audience burst into applause. They gave Paul a standing ovation that went on for a full minute. The judges each held up their paddles — ten, ten, ten. A perfect score! From the audience, the Hoove saw that Billy was looking panic-stricken, so he flipped into hyperglide and zoomed up to the stage.

"Don't look so nervous," he said as he hovered over Billy. "That guy was good, I'll give you that. But never forget the Hoove's Rule Number Two Hundred and Eight. When the going gets tough, the tough get going. We can take this."

"I'm not so sure," Billy whispered.

"I didn't hear that," the Hoove said. "What I heard is YES WE CAN. Now, are you ready to win this thing?"

"I have to get at least all nines," Billy said. "That's hard to do."

"Not for us it isn't," the Hoove said, looking him square in the eye and putting both his pale hands on Billy's shoulders. "Remember, YES WE CAN. Now, let's do it."

As he flew into the audience to take his position next to Tess Wu, his voice echoed around the room with a ghostly howl. "Yyyyesssssss wwweeeeeeeeee caaaaaaaaaaaaaan!"

CHAPTER 15

It took Mr. Wallwetter quite a few minutes of tapping on the microphone to get the kids to settle down.

"I need your attention, people," he repeated over and over. "Our final contestant is waiting. Attention, people. Attention, please!"

No matter what he said, the kids kept applauding and shouting for Paul. Poor Mr. Wallwetter got so frustrated that his mustache actually twitched, which made it look like a very skinny caterpillar was hiccuping on his upper lip. When Paul saw that there was no way Mr. Wallwetter was going to get control of the cheering kids, he spoke into his headset microphone.

"Listen up, you guys," he said. "The other team still has a chance to pull this out. I know I'm a hard act to follow, but show some respect to my man Billy over there."

That made the kids quiet down. Billy barely noticed the noise level dipping and the kids taking their seats. He was deep in thought.

"Our next contestant is Billy Broccoli, who stunned my first-period English class with his amazing feat of mind reading," Mr. Wallwetter said. "Billy, come forward."

Billy walked to the center of the stage staring at his feet the whole time.

"Look up," the Hoove shouted as he hovered in the audience above an unsuspecting Tess Wu. "There's nothing on that floor but wood and scuff marks. Show them your eyes, Billy Boy. Command the room."

Billy didn't even look at Hoover. He couldn't. A feeling was rising up inside his chest . . . a feeling he knew the Hoove wouldn't like one bit.

Mr. Wallwetter spent more time than he needed adjusting the microphone to Billy's height. It was just an excuse to whisper his final instructions in Billy's ear.

"You have to get twenty-seven points for the win," he muttered. "Go for three nines. That's what I'm expecting from you. Nothing less. Hopefully more."

Billy noticed that Mr. Wallwetter's breath smelled like egg salad. He had never been a fan of egg salad.

Mr. Wallwetter took his place in the wings, while Billy stood alone in front of the microphone. He looked out at the sea of expectant faces in the audience. He knew that he and the Hoove could amaze them with their mind-reading trick. But after watching Paul, he realized that their demonstration was exactly that — a trick. What Paul did was real, the result of a lifetime of effort and work and courage. And what was he going to demonstrate?

A trick. A fake. A lie.

"Let's get this show on the road," the Hoove shouted at him. "Open that mouth of yours and commence. You're looking a little pitiful up there."

Billy did open his mouth and commence.

"Does anyone here have a watch with a second hand?" he said.

Samir raised his hand.

"You don't need a watch!" the Hoove shouted. "That's not in the plan. Have Tess stand up. Tell her you're going to read her mind. Get to it, Billy Boy."

"I've changed my topic at the last minute," Billy said. "I have decided to demonstrate my amazing ability to recite the alphabet backward in under fifteen seconds. Samir, I'd like you to time me."

"Nooooooooooo!" the Hoove hollered. "Don't do it, Billy. It's dull. It's boring. Trust me, it is dangerously uncool. You'll ruin your social life forever. There's still time to change your mind."

Billy paused on the stage, thinking carefully about the Hoove's words. He was right. The mind-reading trick was exciting. It was mysterious. It would probably win his team the SOC contest. And it would make him the center of attention at school for a long time to come.

Billy looked at Paul Costello, who gave him a thumbs-up. *He* was a cool guy. Genuinely cool. There was nothing fake about him.

"I'm ready when you are, Samir," Billy said.

Samir looked at his watch, then pointed a finger at Billy.

"Go," he said.

"Don't go!" the Hoove shouted. "I'm begging you."

Billy took a deep breath.

"Z . . . Y . . . X . . . W . . ."

"You're killing me," cried the Hoove. "I was sent here to help you. I'm getting graded on this!"

"N . . . M . . . L . . . K . . . J . . ."

"Now I'm going to be stuck here for all eternity," the Hoove cried. "Thanks a lot, Billy Broccoli."

Billy continued with the alphabet. The Hoove was so furious that he spun around, flipped into hyperglide, and zoomed out of the auditorium.

Billy didn't care. He finished anyway.

"E . . . D . . . C . . . B . . . A!"

A few kids in the audience applauded. Billy saw that most of the applause was coming from Breeze and her friends. He appreciated the support.

"How'd I do?" Billy asked Samir, who was still staring at his watch.

"Nineteen seconds," he answered.

"Ha ha ha! You stink, Broccoli," Rod Brownstone called out from the audience. Some kids around him laughed as well, and Ms. Winter had to go to the microphone and tell them their behavior was inappropriate.

Billy looked over at Mr. Wallwetter as he waited for the judge's scores. The poor man had flopped down into a folding chair in the wings and was nervously tugging at his stringy little mustache. Billy felt bad about letting him down, but he knew he had done the right thing. He walked back to his chair and sat down.

"What happened, dude?" Ricardo whispered.

Before Billy could answer, the judges held up their paddles. Eight. Seven. Eight.

Mr. Wallwetter's head fell into his hands. He was taking it hard. Then he composed himself and walked to the stage, where Ms. Winter was waiting for him at the microphone.

"The final score is Team Wallwetter seventy-one points, Team Winter seventy-four points," he announced. "On behalf of my team, I congratulate the winners — Emily Yamaguchi, Samir Shah, and Paul Costello."

Paul accepted the trophy on behalf of their team, and once again, he got a standing ovation.

"The Wallwetters were great competitors," he told the audience. "Ruby, nice recovery on stage. Billy, impressive try. You'll get it next time. And Ricardo . . . what can I say?"

He rolled over to Ricardo and held up his hand for a high five, one athlete to another.

"Maybe you should stick to baseball, man. That mayonnaise thing was ugly."

Everyone laughed, especially Ricardo.

It was a tradition that the losing team had to stay behind and take the chairs down from the stage. Mr. Wallwetter claimed he had a headache and went back to his room, leaving the kids under the supervision of Mr. Labelle, the school custodian. As they folded up the chairs and carried them to the storage closet, Billy knew he had to explain himself to Ricardo and Ruby.

"So I sort of let you guys down," he began. "I'm really sorry."

"I guess your mind-reading skills weren't working today," Ruby said, gathering up the name tags and putting the plastic holders in the recycling bin. "Is that what happened?"

"They were never really working," Billy said. "I can't read minds. It was a little trick I developed."

"Want to tell us how you did it?" Ricardo asked.

There it was. The question he had been dreading. Billy hesitated. He didn't want to lie, but there was no way he could tell them about the Hoove. Then he remembered a magic show he had seen on television that had interviews with all the great magicians.

"A good magician never reveals his secrets," he told Ricardo, repeating what he had heard the Amazing Cardini say when asked how he did his tricks. He hoped it would be enough to satisfy Ricardo and Ruby. And it was.

"Well, I messed up, too," Ruby said.

"It happens," Ricardo said. "You can't expect to be perfect. Even the great baseball players only get a hit thirty percent of the time."

"So you're not mad at me?" Billy asked Ricardo.

"Forget it, man. Nobody hits a home run every time at bat. By the way," Ricardo said as Billy helped him haul the chairs to the storage closet, "that was a fun sleepover. Maybe we can have another one this weekend. No trips to Dodger Stadium, but we can hang out. Is that cool with you?"

"Very cool," Billy said.

He looked calm on the outside, but inside Billy was jumping up and down. He felt like laughing and crying at the same time. He never knew making friends could be so easy.

CHAPTER 16

When Billy got home from school that afternoon, he headed straight for his room. The hallway had the strong smell of orange juice, so he knew Hoover was nearby, probably waiting to yell at him.

"Hoove," he called once he was safely inside with the door closed. "Come out. I know you're here."

"What's it to you?" came the muffled voice from inside the closet. "It seems my advice is no longer needed by a certain someone who thinks he knows more than I do."

"Don't be a pain. I have stuff to tell you."

"I've already seen this movie, Billy Boy. You made a fool of yourself because you didn't listen to me, and now you want to apologize. That's getting to be a habit with you and me. Well, this time, it's too late. I'm sure the Higher-Ups are writing down the F on my report card as we speak."

"Why would they fail you?"

"In case you forgot, I get graded for Helping Others. You refused to let me help. And if you look bad, I look bad. End of story."

Billy walked over to the closet and pulled the door open. The Hoove was floating in mid-air, his head resting on a stack of T-shirts and his feet draped over the hanger that held Billy's brown dress-up suit pants. He held his hand up to shield his eyes from the sunlight that flooded in.

"Easy there, buddy. My baby blues are going into shock. I left my sunglasses back in the 1940s and have been looking for them ever since."

"Hoove," Billy said. "I didn't look bad. I did fine."

"Did you win?"

"No."

"Then I'm here to tell you, you looked bad."

"Hoove, the other team deserved to win. They were better. And I felt good because I competed the honest way. Without pretending to be something I'm not. I had to do it my way, not yours."

"The fact remains that you ignored me, Billy Boy. Just like the other night when you ignored me and went off with what's-his-name-the-baseball-star to Dodger Stadium. Your new best friend. That hurt me."

"I'm sorry I did that. I didn't realize that it would make you feel so bad. I tried to apologize."

"Yeah, I heard you, when you were having that convo with the squirrel."

"That was you?"

"Who you calling a rodent? I was on the branch above him."

"And you didn't say anything?"

"I wasn't ready. I had a good mind to leave you forever, to tell the Higher-Ups that I'm done trying, that I can no longer be of any help to you."

"So why'd you come back?"

"Met a guy. He said it's not over 'til it's over."

Billy couldn't believe what he was hearing.

"You met Yogi Berra?" he said, his eyes wide with wonder.

"I got friends in high places. Anyway, let's get back to the subject at hand. I think it *is* over between us. You got your new friends. You don't need me. So I'll just be heading out. Maybe there's another kid on the block who needs a personal ghost."

"Wait, Hoove. I got something for you. I want you to have it."

Billy went over to his pink desk and slid open the top drawer. He took out a small silver metal box and handed it to the Hoove.

"Breath mints?" the Hoove said, looking at the box label that showed little blue mints tumbling down a waterfall. "You sure know how to pick swell presents."

"Just open it," Billy said.

The Hoove pried open the lid and looked inside the box. It was filled with dirt, packed down solid all the way to the rim.

"Dirt?" Hoover couldn't hide his disappointment. "You got me a box of dirt. This is how you say thank you and good-bye?"

"It's from Dodger Stadium," Billy said. "I felt so bad that you couldn't go with me that I borrowed this box from Ricardo's uncle. Then I snuck out to the pitcher's mound, dug up some of the ground right next to the rubber, and packed it in here for you. I figured that if you can't go to Dodger Stadium, at least I could bring a little bit of it to you. There's enough dirt there to put your toes in."

Hoover Porterhouse III was rarely at a loss for words. He had a smart remark for every occasion. But as he stood there holding the box that Billy had brought him, he didn't have anything clever to say. He touched the dirt with his transparent fingers.

"This is really from the pitcher's mound?"

"The same one that Sandy Koufax stood on when he pitched that perfect game against the Chicago Cubs."

"September 9, 1965. I remember it well. I watched it on TV. The family that lived here then, the Norberts, still had a black-and-white set. It didn't matter, though. It was a beautiful thing to watch in any color."

For a moment, it was as if the Hoove was a real boy, and he and his best friend were having a conversation about a special moment they both loved.

"I don't get many presents," the Hoove said, closing the little metal box and putting it in his pocket. "But I can tell you right now, Billy Boy, this is the best one I've ever gotten."

He looked toward the window, then back at Billy.

"I wish you'd stay," Billy said. "I could still use your help."

"Well, your wardrobe is pretty weak," the Hoove said. "And your personal grooming definitely needs some improvement. And you have a lot of work to do on that baseball swing. And I can't even go into your fielding right now."

"So?" Billy asked. Even though he only said one word, his voice was filled with nervousness.

"I guess I could give it another shot," the Hoove answered. "And you're going to listen better. Right?"

Billy nodded. "Sit down and I'll show you all the pictures I took for you at Dodger Stadium. Who knows? Maybe one day we'll get to go there together."

"I'd like that," the Hoove said. "No one I'd rather go with."

The two boys were so busy poring over the photos of Dodger Stadium that neither of them noticed the glowing words that were etched with an invisible finger on the window of Billy's room. They said:

Helping Others: B– (but shows improvement).

Can't get enough of Billy and the Hoove?
Read on for a sneak peek at their
next crazy adventure!

GHOST BUDDY

HOW TO SCARE THE PANTS OFF YOUR PETS

Billy awoke with a jolt, not because of the sound of Hoover's voice, but because of the sudden change in Stormy's position. The cat was no longer curled in Billy's lap, but standing on all four paws, her back arched and her mouth open, exposing all her teeth. The hair on her back stood straight up.

"Relax, Stormy," Billy said. "That's just the Hoove. He's your new friend."

Apparently, Stormy didn't think so. She let out a long, low hiss and sprang from Billy's lap, flying through the air in the direction of the Hoove. Her ears were flat against her head and her claws were out. If Hoover Porterhouse had been a real person, she would have landed smack on his chest. But since he was a ghost, she flew right through him and landed on the curtains covering Billy's window. Hissing and growling and showing her teeth, she clutched onto the curtains, never taking her green eyes off the Hoove.

"She's really sweet," Billy called to the Hoove. "Reach out and pet her."

"No way, Billy Boy. In case you hadn't noticed, cats hate me. And I'm not a big fan of theirs either."

"But this is Stormy. She's going to live with us. And you're going to grow to love each other."

The Hoove looked over at the cat dangling from the curtains who was still hissing at him, batting the air with her sharp claws, and showing him her razor-sharp teeth. This sure didn't look like love to him.